COMEBACK

A Gun Pedersen Novel

Leif Enger and Lin Enger

CONTENTS

PRAISE FOR THE GUN PEDERSEN SERIES

COMEBACK

"A well-written, fast-reading thriller. . . . It's got everything."

—*Minneapolis St. Paul Magazine*

"*Comeback* is so good you want to sit down and read it all at once. It's got love and shame and money and the Minnesota woods and lakes, and dark mystery, and a reluctant hero, and it's written with humor and passion."

—Garrison Keillor

SWING

"Solidly entertaining."

—*ALA Booklist*

"In *Swing*, the plot twists as unpredictably as a hangman's rope. *Swing* has muscle (and heart, too)."

—*Alfred Hitchcock's Mystery Magazine*

"[A] sure hit."

—R.D. Zimmerman, author of *Deadfall in Berlin*

STRIKE

"Compelling."

—*Publishers Weekly*

SACRIFICE

"*Sacrifice* is the best novel I've read this year. Not just the best mystery, but the best novel, period."
—Jeremiah Healy, author of the John Francis Cuddy series

"Sharp and engaging!"
—*Minneapolis Star Tribune*

THE SINNERS' LEAGUE

"[A] revelation . . ."
—*Booklist*

BOOKS BY THE AUTHORS

The Gun Pedersen Series, by Leif Enger and Lin Enger:

Comeback
Swing
Strike
Sacrifice
The Sinners' League
Hard Curves

Novels by Leif Enger:

Peace Like a River
So Brave, Young, and Handsome
Virgil Wander
I Cheerfully Refuse

Novels by Lin Enger:

Undiscovered Country
The High Divide
American Gospel

PROLOGUE

1980

On the evening of August 17 something over twenty million people learned of Gunsten Pedersen's sudden retirement from baseball. John Chancellor told them about it on the *NBC Nightly News*, a program not known for its attention to sports figures. Mr. Chancellor did a fair and workmanlike job with the story. He used a tone of sadness, respect for the fallen. He applied a cool network gloss over the sordid parts.

"Major league baseball lost a hero today," he began, "when Gunsten Pedersen, the Detroit Tigers' prized and beleaguered left fielder, walked away from the game." Behind Mr. Chancellor's shoulder a picture of Pedersen appeared, the Topps baseball card from his rookie year. The dark-billed cap with the baroque capital D shaded a young face with high cheekbones and a serious set to the eyes.

"Just three days after attending the funeral of his wife, who was killed in the tragic crash of Flight 347 in Wisconsin, Pedersen told NBC this afternoon he's played his last game.

"The season isn't over, of course, but Pedersen seemed headed for the kind of year most veterans his age can only wish for. He led his teammates in home runs and batting average, and was voted the American League's starting All-Star left fielder for the twelfth time in seventeen seasons. For the past two weeks, though, the normally quiet-mannered Pedersen has been the focus of headlines for his actions off the field. Press reports of his relationship with film star Susannah Duprey"—on screen now, the soundless clip of a sleek, dark-haired woman mouthing words at a thicket of microphones—"were followed by the on-camera fistwork Pedersen performed on a reporter for *The American Mirror*." Another clip flashed on the screen, and a man vast of width took two short blows, to the gut and chin, then rolled sideways onto the hood of a parked car.

The clip ended and John Chancellor was back. "These events shocked a nation of baseball fans. Then came the plane crash. Now it is over. Inside of one week, Pedersen has buried his wife, his career, and a little of the innocence and honor that have always belonged to the national pastime." Chancellor paused, seemed to frown at a paper on his desk. He looked up at the camera. "We asked Mr. Pedersen by telephone what he intends to do now. His answer, and I quote: 'I'm going north.'" A pause. "That's the *NBC Nightly News*. This is John Chancellor. Good night."

1990

Sometimes it seemed like he hadn't gone far enough north.

The first year, living in the log house he'd built for Amanda as a summer place in the early sixties, he'd been tempted to rip the phone out and toss it off the dock into Stony Lake. This was northern Minnesota and his number was unlisted, but people still got it: guys calling up and saying, Get back to the game, man—sorry about your wife, but let's not quit baseball, not the important stuff. Others called to say, You've sinned, buddy, and you're going to hell in a sled you've built yourself. One woman phoned from a group called Females for Fidelity, saying she understood the pressures on professional athletes and was willing to come give him personal support and consolation. He changed his number four times that first year.

It got better after that. He put a new roof on the house, replaced some logs that boarded termites, and made enough quiet trips into the little town of Stony so that people nodded to him now and didn't just stare. Meanwhile the sportswriters found other sensations and misfortunes to use up, and the phone rang less and less often.

He drank coffee in the town bakery sometimes, and the men from the grocery and the hardware store and the bank who always seemed to be there were glad to see him. He started getting phone calls from local politicians. A state representative wanted his endorsement on a school sports bill; the mayor wanted to post a Home of Gunsten Pedersen sign at the Stony city limit. He said no, of course; caution was habitual. Then the Loon Country Attractions thing came up.

Loon Country was the idea of Stony's only certifiable rich man, Lyle Hedman of the Hedman Paper Mill. It would be Minnesota's answer to Disneyland, he said; a high-rise, high-tech island of prosperity in the middle of unemployed northern Minnesota. An amusement park. A convention center. The biggest shopping mall for two hundred miles, any direction. It would sit right next to the big blue water, Stony Lake, and fill the town with business and happiness. Lyle Hedman said so to Gun, and wondered if Gun would like a job putting his face on freeway billboards. Gun said he wouldn't, and then he learned that when it counted, people could still remember the bad stuff.

"You know, Gun, this could be a positive thing for you," Hedman said.

"Positive?"

"Well, yes." Lyle coughed over the phone, and Gun understood. "You had a bit of a rough outing your last time in the public eye."

"No thanks, Lyle."

Then the conservation group called. Save the Lake. They were the ones who worried Loon Country Attractions would send too much sewage and poison into the water. Gun agreed with them. But they remembered too.

"We think your help on this important issue could be beneficial all around. It'll give us a spokesman people will recognize, and give you some very good publicity," the county commissioner said.

"I'm not looking for publicity," Gun told him.

"No, no, but surely it wouldn't hurt, not after . . ."

"Yes?"

"Not after what happened before. Seems to me you'd want to put your name on something folks can respect."

Gun hung up and pulled tobacco and papers from the pocket of his flannel shirt and rolled a smoke at the kitchen table. He toyed with the wooden matches, arranging them there in the shape of a baseball diamond.

Redemption, he realized, might still be a chilly ways distant.

Chapter 1

He stood in the shadow of a white pine, sixty feet six inches from his home-built pitching machine and waited in longjohns and red tennis shoes, the long blond Hillerich and Bradsby resting lightly on his bare shoulder. The metal arm of the machine inched upward, ticking. He relaxed his fingers on the smooth handle as the arm reached horizontal in its rising motion then snapped forward. He took a short stride and swung, his eyes holding the ball until he felt the clean wooden pop, and the line drive took off low, whining. It was still rising when it hit the trunk of a pine tree in what would have been deep left field in a ball park.

"Robbed," he said.

He tapped the flat white stone he used for home plate with the fat end of his bat and rolled his shoulders in a shrug. He never granted himself his morning swim until he'd hit three baseballs into Stony Lake, 380 feet away, never felt ready for a summer day until he'd taken his swings. Every morning as he filled the machine with balls, in his mind he loaded each with something he wanted to forget: Hedman's mall project, his daughter Mazy's anger (which she had every right to), or the mistakes from his old life that people liked to remind him of. Then he watched these freighted balls come floating toward him, and he jacked each one to kingdom come.

He did a deep knee bend, straightened slowly—all six feet, six inches—and rested the bat once more on his shoulder. Again the metal arm ticked upward. He wiggled his bat. From behind came the sound of a vehicle coming up the pitted gravel drive: a creaky, loose-jointed truck, cylinders missing badly. He sighed—that would be

4

Bowser. The metal arm snapped and he strode into the ball. Again the pop of wood on leather, again the rising line drive. Only this time the ball found its way through the sky full of pines, reached its highest point of flight well over the lake, and finally dropped, putting a circular scar in the water's perfect mirror of the sky.

"There." He leaned the bat against the nearest tree and turned to look at the man spilling out the driver's side of a Chevy spotted with rust holes the size of dinner plates.

"Gun Pedersen, Gawd damnit, you owe me!" Bowser Devitz was the son of Jeremy Devitz, and Gun knew his complaint. It was the Devitz property, a hundred sixty acres of low trees and marsh that Hedman had bought for his mall project.

"Gun Pedersen—"

"Yeah, Bowser." Gunsten raised a calming hand.

Bowser marched right up to Gun and stood glaring at him, his face swollen and red, his breath coming hard through his nose. He was forty or thereabouts, and he'd spent nearly all his life in his dad's muskrat swamp. School was his hell, and he'd quit at sixteen with the old man's blessing, and then at eighteen his card got drawn and he pulled up his traps and headed to Vietnam. It was worse than school. He came home in 1971 and moved back in with his dad.

"What's the problem?"

Bowser raised a fist, dropped it. "You're in your skivs," he said quietly. "I don't want to kick a guy who's in his skivs."

"Just finished my swings and now I'm going for a swim." Gun motioned toward the water. "A few baseballs out there to retrieve. I don't suppose this can wait."

"You don't suppose right," Bowser said. He stood

with his big hands curling and uncurling at his sides, apparently uncertain what to say next.

"Okay," Gun said.

"We always liked you, Mr. Pedersen, me and the old man. He used to say you were like us. A guy who wanted to be left alone."

"That's me."

"Not a big shot, like some we know." Bowser took a step forward. Gun felt tired and cold and wished he had his pants on. "So I take it kind of hard that you turn on us that way. And the old man, he takes it even harder."

"I didn't turn on you, Bowser. Your dad could've held on to that land."

"Could've held on to it, like hell. Hedman wanted our piece like you wouldn't believe. The old man, he ain't doing so well."

Rumor had it Jeremy Devitz had sold out so there would be money left after he died, which might be soon. He wanted to protect Bowser. But he might as well have shot him. "Look," Gun said, "you're welcome to stay and talk this over. If that's to your liking, let's go in the house and do it over coffee. Otherwise, I think you should go on home." Gun noticed for the first time that Bowser's eyes looked in two different directions; at the moment, south and southwest.

"I went to see Hedman, see, and he tol' me you're the one I oughta be mad at. He said after he tried buying your land here, you tol' him to go and talk to my dad."

"Not true," said Gun.

"And he said that committee of Tig's—Save the Lake or whatever the hell—he said last month they went and asked you to help buy my dad's property. Save it. All they wanted was a lousy loan, but you said no. If you'da done

6

that, Loon Country woulda been history and maybe you and me coulda worked out some deal so I wouldn't have to move."

"Maybe," said Gun. He felt fatigued, too tired to be explaining himself.

"Fella who'd turn nasty like that to his neighbors oughta have his ass kicked," Bowser went on. "I'm here to kick yours."

"Come in or go home, Bowser." Gun started past him toward the house.

It took a while to get there. As Gun brushed past him, Bowser turned and funneled his three hundred pounds into one fist, aimed low. It connected with the pad of unprepared muscle covering Gun's kidney. It pushed the breath from him and made his legs forget to stand. Gun went to his knees.

"Not so damn tough now, are you?" Bowser stood off to Gun's right, living proof of the strength of large men. "What happened? Gone soft since you quit ball? Only folks you can push around now's a sick old man."

Gun brought air into his body, experimentally, letting it fill his lungs. His kidneys quivered. He felt badly about Bowser, but it wouldn't do to let this go on.

"I gotta tell you, Pedersen. The old man this morning, he got up early and made a big batch of oatmeal." Bowser was waiting for Gun to get back on his feet. He still looked mad. "A great big batch of oatmeal, and I said to him, Geez, Pop, it's just you and me, we're never gonna eat all that."

Gun got up. There were green stains on the knees of his longjohns.

"And Pop says, he's laughing now, he says, It ain't for us, boy, it's for Roxie, she loves it. Roxie! Damn, Pedersen,

Roxie was this old sow we raised for ham back before I went over the pond. Pop sold her for butchering while I was over there. I remember the letter." Bowser's big fists came up as he talked. They shook slightly in front of his chest.

Gun's legs were steadier now and his kidneys felt altered but still whole. He said, "Things are that bad."

"Things have been bad for years. But the sale, Pedersen, that finished it. Pop blinks his eyes and another ten years is gone. He thinks I'm a high school kid. He thinks Ma's just gone into town."

"Let's go inside," Gun said cautiously.

"Bastard!" said Bowser. His lead blow was a right hand square with Gun's breastbone. It filled Gun's lungs with quicksand and he stepped back, twice. Bowser plowed ahead with a windmill left at the solar plexus, but Gun twisted his torso and the blow skipped off. There was a time, Gun realized, when even that first, kidney-burning punch would never have landed. Some animal nerve would have warned him, some movement in the air, and his body would have acted without him. Now that nerve seemed dormant, his defensive reflex tired—though not as tired as Bowser.

"Too old for this . . . are you, Pedersen?" the man said, panting. He moved in with another roundhouse. Gun ducked this one and Bowser slipped on the dewy grass, thumping down butt first. He was breathing heavily now, his face running with sweat. "So . . . you're a ducker," he said. "Shouldn't surprise me. You ducked Loon Country . . . sure as hell." Bowser moved more carefully now, waving his fists like an old-time boxer. Just block the punches, Gun told himself. No more, and certainly no less. Couldn't blame Bowser for feeling this way, after all.

It was just too bad he was so damn strong. Block the fists, and when he's had enough, he'll go on home.

The next one came almost too quick. A left jab, and Gun's right palm deflected it in time to save his nose. Bowser threw another jab, and again Gun slapped it away. A rag of dark hair had flipped down into the big man's eyes and he pushed it back with his knuckles. Gun told him, "Let's quit now."

That brought Bowser's fists in again and Gun fouled off two more jabs like a pair of bad pitches and then let a big right fly past his head, carrying Bowser behind it. The man landed in a full-faced sprawl and lay quiet. Gun left him there and went inside. He made coffee from a red can, boiling it severely on the stove, and then, still in his longjohns, took the pot outside and set it with a mug next to his silent neighbor, who had parked himself on a lawn chair beneath one of the century pines. He was staring west into the cloudless morning.

"You want to talk?" Gun asked him.

Bowser shook his head.

The day was still and a white mist rose up from the lake's unrippled surface, smoke from a cooling battlefield. Gun entered the frigid water without hesitating. He swam forty yards out and dove. The cold ignited a brilliant explosion inside his brain, and he could feel his skin tightening like a wetsuit. It was the middle of May, and the lake had been ice-free for just a few weeks.

Ten feet down, at the sandy bottom, Gun opened his eyes. No walleyes here this morning, no streaks of silver heading for deeper waters. Only refracted spears of light entering from above, penetrating the green haze, dissolving like crystals of salt. He looked around but could not find any baseballs. He kicked for the top.

When he came back in, the lawn and coffeepot were empty, the mug swaying neatly by its handle on the branch of a reaching fir.

Chapter 2

He was on the last phase of his morning workout—push-ups on his fists against the hard kitchen floor—when his second visitor of the day arrived, this time in a pinging four-cylinder with squeaky shocks.

As usual, Mazy shut off the engine and waited for Gun to come outside. He took his sweet time, slowing down the push-ups until they hurt.

Mazy had turned fifteen the week her mother died. Fifteen and needing more from a father than he thought he could give. He'd tried to explain to her that he was afraid, that a ballplayer gone from home seven months a year never learned to be parent enough, never had time, but she knew it all and said it didn't matter. She'd stay, she'd be good, she'd cook and do her homework and keep it all together. Then the aunt in Wisconsin gave Gun what he thought was a better option. She opened those big farmhouse doors for poor motherless Mazy, and he walked her right through, insisting to the last that this was the responsible thing to do. Mazy had ignored the practical, fluttering aunt and said to Gun as he left her, Don't call it responsible. Call it desertion.

Mazy was usually right. It was a troublesome thing.

Now she sat in her dented MG, half frowning at him behind green aviator-style sunglasses. Her thick red-blond hair was chopped off straight at the jawline and her full wide lips were the same shape as her mother's had been, only set harder. She wore a blue chambray work shirt, collar open at the neck, sleeves rolled to the elbows, and the sun was lighting up the silvery hair on her forearms. It stood straight out from her tanned skin, as though electrified.

11

"You're even starting to look like a journalist," Gun said. "Here for an interview?"

His daughter looked off toward the water. Not a muscle moved in her face. "If I were here for an interview, you wouldn't be grinning down at me like that."

"Guess you're right."

"Burger's got a few good stories about you. Sports-writer's nightmare, the way he tells it. 'Forget the crowbar and you'd never get his mouth open.'"

Gun laughed, but Mazy's smile was humorless. And he couldn't tell what her eyes were doing behind those green glasses. "I'll tell him hello for you," she said.

Mazy was twenty-five, and Gun had seen little of her since she turned eighteen. She had gone off to a college in Oregon, then worked for a newspaper in Portland for a couple years before taking the *Tribune* job in Minneapolis. It was good to have her back in the state, but the truth was, she didn't come to see him much. Not that he blamed her.

He leaned against the car and took a lungful of fresh air, tapped a little rhythm on the tight canvas top of the convertible. When the clench in his chest had loosened enough he said, "Come in for breakfast. I'll take my shower and then we can fry up some eggs and bacon. Got some of that good stuff from Harold at the locker. How about it?"

"You know what I'm here about, Dad . . ."

"Come on." He opened the door for her and offered a hand, holding the other behind his back in a gesture of courtesy. Groaning, she took hold of his fingers. He pulled her to her feet. "That's my girl."

"God," groaned Mazy.

Showering, he pictured his daughter moving about in

the bright pine kitchen, cracking eggs and brewing coffee, setting the table with Amanda's old china. He knew perfectly well why she was here. In fact he was surprised she hadn't come sooner.

Already six months had gone by since Gun had signed his property over to her—all four hundred acres, including a quarter-mile of prime lakeshore. At the time, Loon Country had been little more than a rumor. But the phone calls from Lyle Hedman and Tig Larson, the county commissioner, made Gun angry. He'd asked himself, What's a clean, simple way of staying out of things? What do you have to do to make people leave you the hell alone, once and for all? The answer came back. The best thing to do is, you leave.

He told his daughter he wanted to beat the state's inheritance laws. If he should happen to die before his time, she shouldn't have to spend years in the purgatory of probate courts. Reluctantly, she went along with it— she didn't know about Loon Country yet, or not much. So Gun had his lawyer fix it up. Mazy got the land for a tiny fraction of market value, and Gun financed the sale himself. Nothing to it—except from the beginning he knew Mazy would figure out what he was up to.

Now she had, which gave her one more thing to hold against him.

Chapter 3

He walked barefoot into the kitchen, making wet prints on the floor. A wide skylight was cut into the high vaulted ceiling, and beneath it his daughter had breakfast going. Bacon sputtered on the big cast-iron griddle, and eggs sizzled in a copper-bottomed pan. She didn't say a word as he sat down.

She handed him a fully-loaded plate: oven-baked hash browns, three eggs sunny-side up, four strips of thick bacon from the Stony locker, a piece of toast. He got up and went to the stove and poured two cups of coffee from the enamel pot.

They both sat. Mazy looked at him evenly from across the table, her lips turned up in a hard smile. Gun took a gulp of coffee and said, "I hear you've been in town, working."

She nodded.

"And house-sitting for that new editor of the local booster sheet."

"The *Journal*'s not a booster sheet. Not anymore. Have you bothered to take a look since Carol took over?"

Gun shook his head.

"And how do you know where I'm staying? Got Jack spying on me?"

"Honey. It would be a little strange if Jack talked to you and then saw me and didn't tell me what he knew."

She took off her sunglasses and lay them aside. Her brown eyes were tired, bloodshot, and for the first time ever Gun noticed wrinkles in the soft skin beneath them.

"Yeah, okay," she said. "Sorry."

"I am too. I should have told you."

Mazy straightened up. A mean sparkle lit up her eyes.

"That's right—and I would've talked you out of it. Maybe you need a buffer between you and the cruel world out there"—she flung her fingers toward the door—"but it doesn't have to be me. And I don't like being lied to."

"I didn't lie to you."

"You avoided telling me ninety-five percent of the truth."

Gun looked at his hands. He said, "You can do whatever you want with the land. I'm not asking you to save it. You can keep it forever, or you can sell out to Lyle for a million bucks and let him build his giant waterslide. It's up to you. I don't want anybody fighting my battles. All I want is to be left alone. I want to find a place up north as quiet as this used to be. I want to live up there, and I want people to let me be."

"And continue your penance," Mazy said. "Am I supposed to be impressed?"

Gun shook his head. "No."

"Good. I'm sick and tired of your guilty pride, or whatever it is that keeps you out here in the woods."

He lifted his eyes to his daughter's face and leveled his gaze, dropping his voice. "You know what you'd be saying if I'd decided to stay and kill this thing."

"What would I say?"

"That I was throwing my weight around. That I hadn't changed at all. You'd come up with every argument to prove that Lyle Hedman's project is good for the area, good for everybody. You'd make him out to be a philanthropist." Gun took a bite of his egg. "Please tell me I'm wrong," he said.

"You're wrong," said Mazy.

She took a breath and let it out, opened her lips as if to speak, but shut them instead. Then she shook her head and turned her attention to the meal.

When she was finished, she arranged her silverware neatly on her plate—it was something she'd done ever since Gun could remember—and put her green sunglasses on. "None of it makes the least bit of difference," she said. "You know that."

"What do you mean?"

"To Mom," said Mazy. "Or to me, for that matter. None of it makes a difference."

"I'm sorry, Mazy," he said.

He stood and cleared the table, began filling the sink with hot water.

As he'd done thousands of times in the last ten years, he forced a scene into his mind—a nightmare he used against himself: Amanda, home from work and wrapped in a towel, is running her bathwater. She hears the phone and picks it up, expecting Gun's voice, hoping for reassurance that the rumors are just that. But it's another man's voice—a reporter, asking what she feels like, sharing her star.

That evening Amanda had boarded a flight for Minneapolis, where the Tigers were playing the Twins. She was coming, she told him, to hear it straight from the horse's mouth. But she never arrived. Her plane went down in a farmer's cornfield west of Eau Claire.

He shut off the water and pushed up his sleeves past his elbows, took a dishrag from the wooden peg above the sink and submerged a handful of silverware in the suds. Mazy got up from the table and went to the fridge where a stained white towel hung from the door handle.

"People are saying all kinds of things," Gun said. "You've probably heard it already."

"Probably."

"How I'm ducking a fight, siding with the big-money boys, selling out the environmentalists." He rinsed a fistful of silverware and set it carefully in the drain rack.

"Truth is you could have done something, Dad. You could've bought the Devitz land—like Tig's committee asked you to. You could have pulled it right out from under Lyle Hedman's feet. People know that. No land, no Loon Country."

"Jeremy needs every cent he can get out of that swampland," said Gun. "Lyle gave him top dollar."

"Jeremy would've let it go for half the price to save this lake."

"Yeah, and then Lyle would have gone after someone else's land and people would've asked me to buy that too."

"Maybe."

Through the window Gun watched a high range of mountain-blue clouds advance from the west and put a hard slate surface on the water. He was nearly finished washing the dishes when Mazy spoke again. "Are you going to the benefit tonight?"

"What's that?"

"The Hedmans are throwing a dinner and dance, proceeds to the paper-mill workers who've been laid off."

"Yeah? Pretty strange, considering Hedman laid them off."

"It was Geoff's idea."

"Good for him."

"Geoff has . . . changed," said Mazy. Something shifted in her voice.

"Jack tells me you've been spending time with him."

Mazy turned and gave him a look. "That's none of your concern."

He lifted both hands and held them palms out in front

17

of his chest. "All right, okay."

She dried a plate, moving her head in a circle, as if trying to work out the kink. "I was wondering, how about going with me? Somebody wants to meet you."

"I've already met Geoff."

"Funny. I'm talking about Carol Long. She's getting back into town tonight."

"Actually, I'm driving north this afternoon to look at some land and won't be back until late."

"Fine, then." Mazy dropped her towel on the counter and walked to the door. As she swung open the screen, Gun spoke her name. She stopped on the threshold and turned, her face inscrutable. He tried to smile.

"Just tell me there's nothing between you and Geoff," he said. "Tell me you're only using him to get at the story."

She worked her hands into the tight front pockets of her Levi's. "I'm only using him to get at the story," she said, and then left, slamming the door behind her.

Standing at the sink, he watched his daughter walk to her car. The sway in her stride was the same as her mother's, and she held her head cocked to the right, as if listening to a quiet voice. She started it up, turned it around, and drove out of sight around the bend in Gun's rutted driveway.

He realized his phone was ringing.

Chapter 4

He picked it up and said, "Yeah?"

"God, I'm glad you're there!"

"Who is this? Tig? You don't sound so good."

"I'm awful. Could you please—" His voice broke into a cough and he grabbed a breath that sounded like a straw sucking the bottom of a glass.

"What's going on?"

"You'll understand when you get here. Please." The receiver clicked and he was gone.

"I'm on my way, Tig."

Tig Larson, county commissioner, treated life itself as an emergency, and so Gun didn't feel the need to hurry. He walked out to his pickup, a white F-150, its windshield the victim of a wicked foul ball. When he turned the key, the engine backfired then started up in a ragged rhythm that shook the cab. He waited for all eight cylinders to find their balance, then turned a circle around home plate and followed his daughter's tracks.

Tig lived on the other side of the lake in a cluster of suburban-type homes, and Gun took the long way around instead of through town, following the narrow lake road and driving with his window down, enjoying the breeze off the water. Most likely the commissioner had worked himself into a state of nerves about the referendum next week. He was probably out to make a last ditch effort to enlist Gun's help. Nothing new.

His home was small and neat and built into the south side of a hill, and this morning he had pulled the dark shades down on his floor-to-ceiling windows. When Gun knocked, Tig opened just a crack and peered out over the chain of the safety lock.

"You okay?" Gun asked. The man's face was fish-belly white.

Tig groaned. "Thank you for coming." He opened up. "Here, I'll get us a drink," he said, reaching for the bottle on his big console television.

"No thanks."

Tig poured himself half a tumbler of brandy and drank it straight off.

"What's going on?"

The man pointed outside and told Gun to follow him. He led the way out the door and down the slope twenty yards to a small wooden storage shed, stopped just short of it and wiped at his eyes with the knuckles of both hands. "In there," he said.

Gun went in. There weren't any windows, and it was too dark to see, but there was a distinct smell in the close air—an unhealthy smell. "You got a light in here?"

"The wall to your right."

He flicked the switch and found himself staring into the wide bloody eyes of a cat, a yellow tabby. It blinked twice and made a sound like a child clearing its throat. "Hoo," Gun breathed. The cat was spread out wide and staked against the wall, nails driven through all four paws. It was sliced open from throat on down, loops of multicolored entrails hanging to the floor.

"Still alive," Tig moaned.

Gun stepped from the shed, thinking of himself at thirteen and having to shoot his big Newfoundland dog Sally after she got hit on the road by the mailman's car. He'd used the twelve-gauge at close range, quick and painless, and hadn't cried until he dragged her off into the woods for burial and felt the dead weight of her. Now he walked past Tig to the pickup truck, took the .38 Smith &

Wesson from underneath the seat and came back.

"Oh, God," said Tig. Gun rested a hand briefly on the man's shoulder.

He was careful to plug one ear with a finger and turn the other away, but the sound was still deafening inside the small structure. The cat relaxed, its head drooped, and there was a small new hole of sky in the wall. Gun found a hammer and removed the nails, then took the animal down and buried it in the scrub weeds beyond Tig's lawn.

"Terrorism, plain and simple," Tig was saying. "Can't you see? Hedman's trying to turn me around, mess with my head. The man's paranoid. He's got all the money in the world, he's got the support of everybody with influence, and he's still afraid he's gonna lose. He's been out here to visit me half a dozen times in the last month. And last time he got angry."

"What are you asking me to do?" Gun shook his head when Tig offered the bottle, watched as the man refilled his own glass.

"Aw, damn, I don't know. It's getting late in the game. Would have been nice if there was somebody else on my side, taking some of the heat. Somebody like you. Somebody who wouldn't back down. I thought you were the sort of guy that comes through in a jam. Not somebody who runs off, you know?"

Gun got up to leave. "You'll have to handle it alone, Tig."

"You wanna see Hedman win, is what I think. You stand to make a little cash on the deal."

Gun leaned forward, raising an eyebrow, "I think this plan of Hedman's sucks. Same as you do. But there's a lot of folks around here who don't agree."

"Who? Tell me who."

Gun sat back down. "The guy laid off from Hedman's mill, say. Got a bunch of kids at home and his wife's waiting on tables. The boys on Main Street . . ." Gun stopped himself. He'd never been a bullshitter and it was too late to start.

Tig laughed. "You'd make a lousy politician, know that?"

Gun rose to his feet again and moved to the door. "That's right. Plenty of those types running around already. Let them fight it out. People like yourself and Reverend Barr. Summon your forces and have your little war and see who comes out on top. That's how these things work. I don't want any part of it."

Tig drained off another glass and laughed bitterly, shaking his head. "I've heard people say this before about you, Gun, but I never wanted to believe it."

"What's that?"

"Lack of loyalty. You watch out for the big slugger, numero uno, and to hell with the rest of them. Guess your wife could have said something about that."

Gun felt like he'd been dealt a punishing blow to the gut. He took a deep breath, turned, and opened the door. "She could at that," he said, and left.

That afternoon he drove north as he had planned, but the property he was thinking of buying didn't look nearly as good this time. Partly it was the rain that had moved in. It came down hard and steady and smelled like fish. The air was still, not a trace of wind, and everywhere Gun looked he saw the same miserable gray concoction of heavy weather he was feeling inside.

Chapter 5

Next morning he was in his kitchen, toweling off after a swim, when someone rapped three quick beats on the door.

"Come in."

"Mr. Pedersen?" The door opened and a woman stepped in, no one he knew. She wore black jeans, long ones, and black pumps that bared tan ankles to the chill of morning. She had black bangs with a few gray strands scattered over her forehead, lake-green eyes Gun found himself wanting to look good for.

"Sorry about the longjohns," he said.

She smiled, an easy tropical smile, then turned it down some and said, "I'm Carol Long. Your daughter's been watching my place for me."

"Yes." He shoved his wet hair back with his fingers, and a cold cup of Stony Lake ran down his spine. "Mazy's mentioned you. You met at that reporters' thing in Minneapolis."

"The symposium, right." The smile left and a little fluster came into her voice. "Mazy's not here."

"She should be?"

"I was hoping so. I couldn't get back last night, so I called her, asked her to stay on an extra day. I pulled in half an hour ago, and she's gone. Thought she might be over here."

Gun finished with the towel and pointed to the stove. "There's coffee. Mind if I put some clothes on?"

He went to the bedroom and wondered what she was doing, coming out here like this. Not even eight in the morning. Must be something important if she was in such a hurry to find Mazy. There were nerves in her voice.

Nothing nervous about the way she moved, though, Sweet Heaven no. Gun wondered if she knew how she looked to him; those slim black jeans, that smile, probably she did. He wondered how he looked to her, a man edging past the middle years, in goosebumps and soaking longies. Hair going white before its time. He shut it from his mind and found gray wool socks, jeans, a red wool shirt. It was cool in the house.

She was at the kitchen table ignoring a cup of coffee and nibbling at a silver-set emerald on her left hand. Gun poured and sat down.

"Now," he smiled, "what's so important you've got to come chasing my girl before breakfast gets cold?"

"Mr. Pedersen, it's not that. Listen. She was supposed to stay at my house through today. We talked about it. Now I drive in, early, she's nowhere in sight. There's her typewriter, even some notes lying next to it, a blank sheet rolled in. Her car's in the drive. But she's not there."

"She runs in the mornings sometimes," Gun said. "Two, three miles, farther once in a while."

Carol Long cleared her throat. Her eyes met Gun's and he saw a spark of steel in them. "Mr. Pedersen. Do you know why I wanted someone in my house while I was gone?"

"It's Gun. No, I don't."

"I've had some trouble with vandals. And I was threatened."

"It's a virus around here lately," Gun said.

"So far just a few well-chosen words spray-painted across my picture window, but I got a phone call promising worse. I suppose you can guess what it's about."

"Mmm. I could."

"You do read the *Journal*, I suppose."

"I'm sure it's a good paper," said Gun.

Carol stiffened, then said, "I've been running editorials against the Loon Country development."

"Hedman wouldn't appreciate that." Gun lifted his coffee, looked at Carol over the cup. "Did Mazy know why you wanted somebody at your place?"

"Of course. Look, she's been poking around enough to get some people upset. Good reporters do that. I just thought . . ." She let the sentence die on the table.

"You think she got somebody upset enough to do something damn stupid," Gun said. "All right. Let's be sensible. You say her car's still there, her typewriter. What about her other stuff, clothes and things?"

Carol looked at Gun, red coming up under her tan. "God, I didn't even look, I didn't think. I'm sorry, it just seemed so weird and empty in the house, that old IBM of hers humming on the table all by itself—I came straight out. I thought maybe you'd picked her up, spur of the moment, go get some breakfast, I don't know." She stood abruptly and went to the door. Gun followed.

"I live twenty minutes from here. I'll call you." Carol smoothed her hair.

"She'll probably be there waiting for you," Gun said. "Don't worry, Mrs. Long."

"Not Missus," Carol said, and went.

In his kitchen he opened a drawer and removed a narrow red can of tobacco and a match-book of papers. He rolled a cigarette, lit it, then sat at the table to smoke. The clock above the fridge said a quarter of eight. Between drags he twirled the cigarette like a baton in his big fingers and blew smoke rings at the open-beam ceiling. He told himself his daughter knew how to take care of herself, that she wasn't a kid anymore, that she was smart enough to keep people from feeling threatened, that she knew how to put folks at ease, unlike most journalists Gun knew. And he'd known too many. Anyway, she was probably out running.

The phone rang and he picked it up. "Hello."

"Carol Long." Her voice was low and controlled now. "I checked in the bathroom, and her makeup and toothpaste and cosmetic case, they're all there. But it's strange. I checked the bedroom, the dresser and closet. Most of her clothes are gone, underwear, socks, jeans, all six pairs—I was talking to her when she unpacked. Her suitcase too. She shoved that under the bed, and it's not there now. Mr. Pedersen, Mazy left in a hurry. I think you'd better call the police."

He shifted the receiver from one ear to the other and started rolling a new cigarette. "Carol, didn't Mazy tell me you've been a reporter in Hawaii for the last twenty years?"

"That's right."

"I suppose over there people call the cops when they think someone's in trouble. Here in Stony it's not that simple."

"Oh?"

"How well are you acquainted with the police here—Chief Bunn?"

Gun waited while Carol drew a slow breath. "He seems . . . competent enough."

"Really?"

"Yes."

Gun put the unlit cigarette between his lips, took his time, reached for a kitchen match. "Carol, I shouldn't, but I'm going to tell you a story. True one." He scratched the match on the black burner of the stove. He lit the cigarette and waved the match out. "You know Harley Arnold, the grocer."

"Sure."

"He's a neighbor of Bunn's half a mile or so down the road. A few winters ago he caught a couple fool kids from the high school swiping cooking sherry from his shelves. He called their folks. Couple nights later somebody drove past his house and put half a dozen .22 slugs in his cedar siding."

Carol was quiet.

"So Arnold called Bunn, and Bunn came over the next night to see if anyone would try it again. He parked the police car behind a big snowdrift a block from Arnold's, and he waited in Arnold's junipers for three hours."

"Okay."

"While he was waiting, those same fool kids came along and took the police car for a ride. Parked it in some frozen rushes out on the lake. He'd left the keys in it."

"All right. But at least he gave it a try. He could've done worse."

"He did worse. At eleven o'clock he said good night to Arnold and went on home. Walked home. Forgot he'd ever brought the car. He didn't notice it was gone until the next morning, and it was a week before anyone found it." Gun tapped ashes into the sink. "There's nothing bad about Chief Bunn, Carol. He just ought not to be a cop."

"I see." Carol paused. "What about Sheriff Bakke? Have you got a reason not to call him?"

"We don't have time for another story."

"So. You're going to take care of this yourself."

"That's right. Good-bye, now, and thanks for the call." He hung up, finished dressing, went outside and started his truck. He didn't hurry. Between his heart and stomach he could feel something cool and hard and buoyant, like an icy balloon, a familiar feeling, and an old one. During his seventeen years with the Tigers he'd had it often, usually in the late innings when he came to bat with men on base. A good number of his 426 home runs had floated out on the icy balloon. Gun thought of it as a gathering place of his energy, concentration, and nerve. It put his brain on automatic, sharpened his senses. Since leaving the game ten years ago, though, the feeling had been absent. Now it was back, and Gun was grateful for its return.

Chapter 6

He went south on the lake road and headed toward Stony, population 3,415, where the year-round people lived in modest wood-frame houses and either worked at the Hedman Paper Mill or lived off tourism and unemployment.

Two miles from town he stopped at a small tavern nearly hidden by a dense stand of birches, lake glittering in the background. A neon sign blinked from a window, bright green: JACK BE NIMBLE'S, it said. Gun parked in the lot and walked in. Knotty pine walls all around, darkly golden in the morning light, and behind the gleaming mahogany bar, Jack LaSalle, short and thick with a black crewcut and a face like the rough bust of a Roman stoic, not a soft feature in it. "You're early," Jack said. He set a cup of black coffee on the bar. "Twins beat your Tigers, twelve-eight."

"Only way they can win. No pitching."

"Sour grapes."

"Have you seen Mazy?" Gun asked.

"Um, yeah. Day before yesterday, I believe it was. In the evening."

"Alone, was she?"

Jack opened his mouth, froze, then shook his head. "Geoff," he said.

Gun stared ahead into the mirror behind Jack's assortment of bottles. He didn't like what he saw, eyes too deep inside their sockets, hollow cheeks, pinched mouth. He looked old.

"Let's hear it," Jack said.

"Mazy's gone." He told him about his argument with Mazy yesterday and Carol Long's visit this morning, his own rising concern. "I'm worried," he said.

Jack wiped at a spot on the bar. "Damnit, Gun, I didn't think anything of it, Mazy and Geoff—figured she was getting her story for the paper, pumping him for the inside stuff."

"She seemed okay?"

Jack pointed across the room. "They were in that booth. Geoff looked pretty eager, sure, sitting up straight like a pup. Bought some wine, made his little moves—you know Geoff."

"And Mazy?"

Jack shook his head. "Friendly enough to keep him talking, cool enough to keep him honest. Or that's how it looked to me. Gun"—Jack lifted a blunt finger—"if I'd thought she was having trouble with him, I'd have broken his ass."

"I know that," Gun said.

"She knew what she was doing, I'm sure of it. I didn't want to put the chill on her interview."

Gun shifted on his stool and tapped his cup on the bar. "I think I'll take a little drive out to Lyle's place," he said. Then finished the last of his coffee and got to his feet.

"You need any help, you know where to look," Jack told him.

***

It was the year after the accident, Mazy sixteen and spending the summer with Gun, when he'd paid his first visit to Lyle Hedman. On that August night Mazy was having a party in the woods north of the house, and Gun put up a big canvas tent for the girls to sleep in. Then at one a.m. he'd woken to screams he could feel between his ears like razor-wire, and he pulled on his pants and ran toward the tent, a couple hundred yards north of the house. Before he reached it, he saw a flash of movement in the trees and flattened himself on the ground. No sounds came from the tent, no movement anywhere. Then a shout from Gun's left and two young men in swim trunks and Halloween masks charged from the trees. They ran straight for the tent, throwing what looked like tomatoes or apples as they came, the missiles thumping the canvas. The girls screamed. Then one of the boys yelled, "Sharon's turn!" and they both pushed through the tent's canvas doorway. After a few seconds of scuffling, they emerged with one of the girls, Sharon Turner, whose voice rose like a siren. She was overweight and wore white pajamas, and the boys had her by the arms and legs, her bottom dragging on the ground.

"Hey, Geoff!" This from Frankenstein, who aimed a flashlight toward the trees. Like magic, a naked body appeared, jumping, twisting, and goose-stepping over the grass. The streaker wore a Jimmy Carter mask and headed straight for the shrieking girl. As he came, the two boys holding Sharon flipped up her pajama top, exposing her, and the streaker—at the last instant—veered off and disappeared into the trees, howling.

Gun sprinted for the boys, who let go of Sharon and ran. He knew where they'd likely parked, though, and he intercepted them before they reached their car. Two fled on foot, but Gun managed to hang onto the third— grinning Jimmy Carter—and he tore off the boy's mask. It was Geoff Hedman, twenty-one-year-old son of Lyle. The car belonged to him, a new Jag, and Gun found the keys in the ignition and told Geoff to get in, he'd drive him home. Geoff scrambled into the backseat, head down, and shucked into his clothes.

The Hedman house was a massive structure built of redwood logs imported from the Northwest, low-hanging eaves extending steeply to a high peak. That night the long drive was lined with gas torches, their flames wavering in the breeze off the lake. The windows of the lodge blazed. Cars were parked bumper to bumper along the drive. Gun pulled up beneath a flickering torch. He said, "We're going in together, Geoff, and you're going to do something for me."

"I swear, Mr. Pedersen, it wasn't my idea. I didn't want to do it. I'm sorry." Geoff had been apologizing nonstop for ten minutes. "We were just out for some fun, give 'em a little scare."

"You scared them, all right. And now you're going to have some fun. You're going to tell your old man what you and your friends were doing out there."

Without knocking, he opened the door and brought Geoff inside, where they stood on the welcome mat, Gun gripping the young man's arm. Geoff tried to crouch and cower, but Gun held him straight. In the center of the room a stuffed African elephant—a trophy from Hedman's recent safari—was frozen in mid-bellow, tusks lifted toward the ceiling. Beneath it Hedman and his wife held court, nodding and smiling at a pressing cluster of guests. Throughout the room people formed intimate knots, heads moving agreeably with drink. At first no one noticed them standing there, but then Hedman's eyes wandered toward the door and flashed open wide. His wife, then the people near him, and finally the whole crowd turned.

In the silence Geoff moaned.

Gun spoke quietly. "Lyle, your son wants to tell you

32

what he and his pals have been up to."

Chapter 7

So this was Gun's second visit to Hedman's place, the first in daylight. He turned off the lake road six miles north of Stony, at a black sign shaped like an elephant with tusks lifted. A hundred yards in, a gate with iron bars blocked the drive. Gun stopped his truck and got out. The gate hadn't been here nine years ago. Neither had the twelve-foot, chain-link fence that reached away in both directions.

Behind the gate was a young man wearing an orange sleeveless jumpsuit, five-ten, weight-lifter's build, a .38 holstered at his side. Gun took from his trouser pocket a receipt for two hundred-pound bags of cement he'd purchased from Darwin's Lumber in Stony and he folded the receipt twice.

"Hello," Gun said.

"You call ahead?" asked the guard.

"No reservation, sorry."

"Hedman doesn't have time for walk-ins."

"Fine, I'll give you a note for him." Gun moved up to the iron gate, reached his hand through the bars and offered the folded receipt. "Make sure he gets it."

When the guard's fingers touched the receipt, Gun seized his wrist and yanked him hard against the bars, the man's head knocking the iron like a block of wood. He grabbed him by the hair, and maintaining a steady pull, reached through the bars and drew the gun from its holster. Then he let the man go.

"Open the gate," he told him.

Rubbing his crown, the guard sorted through his circle of keys and opened the lock.

"Now," Gun said, "if you want to look like a monkey in

front of your boss, come with me. If not, start running toward Stony. It's that way." He pointed with the .38.

The orange-suited guard glanced up briefly, then started down the road.

Behind Hedman's big house, Stony Lake was choppy, blue-black waves capped with gray foam. Gun parked the truck and was about to walk to the front door when he spotted Hedman down by the water, on his long floating pier. He was stowing gear on one of his boats and he didn't look up until Gun stepped onto the pier, rocking it slightly.

Hedman smiled. "Well, Gun." He picked up the tank and stepped into the black and gold bass boat. A long, skinny man, his movements flowed like water.

"Lyle," Gun said.

Hedman stood on the floor of the boat, hands on hips. His fleshy face belonged on a heavier body, and he kept it cocked to the left, showing Gun only the right side. "You going to shoot me?" he said. He was looking at the .38.

Gun tossed it to him. "You're not an easy guy to drop in on."

From the prow of the boat came a low rumble. An Irish wolfhound sat there motionless, its face bearing an expression of intelligence and gravity. The dog's eyes were the same color as Hedman's, the shade of watery beer.

Hedman laughed. "Don't mind Rupert, he's obedient."

"I'll bet he is."

"And about the weapon"—Hedman held up the .38 with two fingers—"believe it or not, we need them here." He spoke in an easy sibilant tone. "Trouble with vandals."

"Funny," said Gun. "I heard the same thing from Tig Larson and Carol Long."

Hedman smiled again. "A beautiful woman, Ms. Long." He brought his hands together. "What brings you out here? You're a man known for preferring his own company."

"A visit."

"I'm going fishing. Come along?"

"You like to talk on the water?"

"Untie us," said Hedman.

Gun freed the lines and stepped aboard. In five minutes they were anchored off the northwest shore of Hambone Island, out of the wind, and Hedman was casting out and reeling in smoothly, the rod like an extension of his arm. Watching him, Gun saw that his left eye was bruised, the flesh around it covered in make-up.

"Somebody hit you?" Gun asked.

Lyle's quick laugh wasn't convincing. "Hit myself. Had my truck up on the lift, wrench slipped on the goddamn oil plug. Hurt like a bastard."

"Always change your own oil?" Gun asked.

"Damn right!" Hedman flared.

"Admirable," Gun said.

Lyle glared at him, then looked suddenly toward his line and set the hook. The fish didn't put up much of a fight—a small pike—and Lyle tossed it back in.

"You know what I'm here about," Gun said as Hedman rebaited his hook.

"Why don't you just tell me and then I'll know for sure."

"My daughter seems to be missing, and I hear she was with your kid the other night."

Hedman's face didn't show a thing. His beer-colored eyes blinked a couple times. "Gun, I'm sure you remember that night you brought Geoff home. I was damn unhappy at the time, I don't mind telling you. But after I learned the details—and cooled off a little—I understood what you did. Appreciated it." He cast in his line, then reached out and patted Rupert's large head.

"Mmm," said Gun.

"No, and I learned a lesson."

"What was that?"

"That it's damned hard to acknowledge that you've lost touch with your own kid."

"I came here to talk about Mazy."

"Hear me out. Truth is, Geoff and Mazy went out together last night, and it wasn't the first time." He smiled, flashed his eyebrows. "Gun, our kids—"

"Mazy's on a story," Gun said.

Rupert made his presence known with a rumble, and Hedman stroked his neck.

"You're grievously mistaken, Gun." Hedman's eyes slid to starboard, where a Frisbee-sized turtle swam parallel to the boat, five or six feet away. He picked up a landing net from beneath his seat, eased it into the water behind the turtle, and thrust forward, snaring it. Then he dumped it upside down on the floor of the boat. Its underside was waxy, and mottled in a geometric pattern of Halloween orange and sea green. Its legs clawed at the air.

Hedman looked up. "You're wrong about your daughter and my son. As for Mazy's interest in Loon Country Attractions, I have nothing to hide. She was free to look at my records, and I might add that her understanding of the project's economic implications far exceeds yours."

"Where the hell is she?"

"I don't know. And I don't know where Geoff is, for that

matter. But I can sure guess who he's with. Last week he told me . . . Well, he didn't come out and say it, but I think it's safe to say they're planning on—what do you call it? Running off together. It's not like they're kids anymore."

"Cut the shit."

The dog growled again, low thunder rising from its massive chest.

"Don't believe me then."

"I don't."

"Fine. But Geoff hasn't been home since yesterday, and I haven't seen or heard a thing." With his toe Hedman nudged the turtle, which had managed to right itself.

"Mazy hasn't run off with your kid. And if this has something to do with your development scam, I'll find out."

"Of course," said Lyle. "But my inclination is to believe that you and I are soon to be relatives." He flipped the turtle over again, then took a toad stabber from his fishing box and sliced the turtle's craning neck, shell to mouth. Then he tossed the turtle in the water and it sank in a cloud of its own blood. Rupert whined and bumped his nose nervously against the gunwale of the boat.

"Always hated turtles," Hedman said. "One bit me once, right here." He held up his right thumb to display a tiny white scar.

Gun said, "How about cats, you hate them too?"

"Depends on whose cat it *is*." Behind the automatic smile, Hedman's face glistened with an emotion that looked for all the world like fear.

Chapter 8

"Bullshit. I don't care what the bastard says, I know what I saw, and it wasn't a pair of love-birds."

Gun had driven from Hedman's straight to Jack's. It was eleven-fifteen, and after telling his friend what he knew, he'd ordered breakfast and then eaten it, silent, while Jack vented.

"Lyle's full of shit, always has been," said Jack.

Gun finished his glass of buttermilk. His friend didn't know of the land transfer, and Gun wasn't about to say anything. Not yet. Nothing he said would make any difference now. The fact was, if Mazy had married Geoff, the Hedmans had managed to get their hands on the best land they could ever hope to ruin.

"I mean, what would they want with her, anyway? You think she came up with something embarrassing and they found out? Or something illegal?"

"It's possible," Gun said.

"But Hedman's not crazy enough to . . . I don't know, Gun. Damnit, what in the hell is going on?"

"Hedman sure acts like he knows."

"You don't believe that rubbish any more than I do." He took Gun's plate and glass and set them on the counter behind the bar. "And hey, the referendum might not pass anyway."

"No?"

"Fifty-fifty, I'd say. Doesn't help, of course, that Reverend Barr jumped on the bandwagon. And that mock-up of Loon Country in the bank lobby—have you seen it?"

Gun shook his head, rubbed his jaw. He hadn't shaved yet, and it was about time he did. Go home, clean himself up, get his head together, take a few swings. He lifted a hand and started for the door, then thought of something else and turned. "What if there's somebody bigger than Lyle, putting pressure on him?"

"What do you mean?"

"What I told you about Tig's cat?"

"What about it?"

"We don't know Lyle was behind it, but say that he was. Seems like a desperation move."

"Filthy lucre," said Jack.

"And something else. I think somebody knocked Lyle around a little bit, put the fear of God in him." He told Jack about Hedman's bruised face.

"Who are you thinking?"

"I don't know," Gun said, "but I'm damn sure going to find out." He went to the door but it opened as he reached for the knob, and Carol Long was there. She'd changed into khaki shorts and a Hawaiian shirt.

Jack called from the bar, "Carol, you brought your legs."

She smiled at Gun. "He isn't well."

"Observant, though," Gun said.

She tilted a look at him and glided over to the bar. "Sorry I sprang in on you that way this morning. Have you learned anything?"

"I'm learning."

"Onerous process," said Jack.

"Well, I'm glad I found you. I happened to run into Reverend Barr at Fisher's Café this morning. Talkative man. You might be interested."

"Yeah?"

Carol shook back her hair like a schoolgirl. It was straight and black, except for the rare gray strands that twisted off course, erratic pencil lines of light. "He asked if I thought my editorials were doing any good, and I told him yes, I hoped so, and then he gave me this foolish grin, looked around, and whispered, all high-stakes intrigue. 'I suppose you've heard about Hedman's new land deal,' he said. I said no I hadn't, and he said, 'Well, it's no rumor —Lyle's got an iron-clad guarantee on Stony Lake's best property.'"

Jack's face was as hard as the mahogany bar that reflected its image. His dark eyes, fastened on Gun, didn't blink. "What the hell's he talking about?"

Carol watched him too.

Gun didn't answer. From Jack's kitchen a country-western tune crackled through poor reception. Either Mazy had said nothing to Carol about the land transfer, or else Carol was playing dumb. But the lines in her forehead looked earnest. "I think you'll be finding out soon enough," he said, then he tipped his head toward Carol Long and walked out of Jack Be Nimble's into aspen shade and brilliant splotches of noon sun.

Chapter 9

The bells at Reverend Barr's church were doing their post-service chiming as Gun approached the edge of Stony. On impulse, he turned off Main Street and guided his truck along First Avenue toward the high-steepled edifice of red brick. He double-parked in front of it, sat with his elbow out the window, watching the parishioners file out the church doors and down the steps. Reverend Barr pumped hand after hand, often leaning close to offer words of flattery or wit, judging from the responses: nods or shakes of head, embarrassed shrugs, tossed hands. Gun wondered how Barr had managed to squeeze Loon Country into his sermon this week. Last week, Gun had been told, Barr had used the parable of the talents, the great New Testament defense of capitalism.

Now Barr was shaking County Commissioner Tig Larson's hand. Larson had a stiff smile and an anxious set to his shoulders. He escaped quickly, and as he turned onto the sidewalk Gun eased the truck forward and pulled up alongside him.

"Hey, Larson."

Larson didn't slow down.

"Larson!"

Larson turned, pointing at his watch. "Sorry, Gun, I'm in a hurry. If you don't mind . . ."

"No problem." Gun accelerated, watching Larson in his rearview mirror.

Back on Main Street, Gun headed west. He had made a mistake, signing his property over to Mazy, that was clear enough. But the deed was done, and the question now seemed to be whether she had transferred the land to Hedman willingly. Had she been forced into marrying

Geoff, or was it her own free choice? For that matter, were they married at all?

He swerved to miss a squirrel, then down-shifted and turned north on the lake road and gave the big eight-cylinder some gas, shifted back into fourth.

No, he couldn't imagine it, couldn't squeeze the two of them into the same frame. Impossible. If his daughter was married to Lyle Hedman's son, it wasn't because she wanted to be. A chill shook Gun and it tingled in his fingertips. He spoke aloud, in order to convince himself. "She wouldn't," he said. As he steered the Ford along Shipman's Bay he caught sight of old Leo Hardy, alone for the last quarter century, standing tall and mackinawed on his dock. Leo waved, and Gun tapped two hoots on the horn. It was a little like looking at himself.

It hadn't been easy, giving Mazy up, and it hadn't taken long to see his error. Her visits home were frequent, but she always went out of her way to let him know he'd been wrong, letting her go. And now, bumping along the rutted drive, he asked himself if maybe she resented him even more than he'd known. He parked the truck next to the garage and stepping out onto the uncut grass heard the faint jingle of the phone ringing in his kitchen. By the time he got there, it was too late. He rolled a cigarette and sat down to smoke it. The phone would ring again.

When it did, on his third cigarette, he picked it up.

"Dad?"

"Mazy. Tell me you're all right."

"I'm fine, great, just . . . fine."

"Where are you? It's Sunday . . . I mean, we've been wondering where you are."

"With Geoff. Out at Hedman's. Got here this morning. In fact I just missed you, according to Lyle."

"What are you doing?" He had to ask, he had to hear her say it.

"Dad?" The pitch of her voice was higher than usual. The tone all wrong. Harder. Her sentences shorter. "Dad, Geoff and I . . . we're married. We eloped, last night."

So, there it was. "You don't sound the same."

"I'm fine. Please. I'll come and visit—or no, why don't you come out here? Lyle says to tell you that you're always welcome. In fact, why don't you—"

"Tell me who it was that married you. Where'd you go?"

She said nothing.

"Tell me who married you and Geoff. I have to know."

"I don't know his name. A civil wedding, Ojibwe County. The old guy that runs the hardware store in Blackstone. Something Gordon?"

"Sweetie, I'll do what I can, you know that. I'll do whatever I have to do." Gun was fingering the tobacco papers, but he didn't roll one.

"Drive out here," Mazy said. "Do that, okay? And about the land—"

"Forget the land, Mazy. Forget it."

"I've got to go. We'll talk later. We're about to have dinner. Fresh walleye." She gave a little laugh that sounded almost cynical.

Gun was silent.

"Dad, I love you."

"You too," said Gun. "You know that."

"I've got to go now, okay?"

"Good-bye, honey. Don't worry now, all right?"

"'Bye now."

"All right?"

She hung up.

He knew it wasn't any use but he made the call anyway. Zeke Gordon was pushing ninety, cataracts on both eyes, the sort of man whose proximity to the next world puts soft colors on the present one. Every time Gun had seen him, the man was shedding happy tears about something. New kittens in the alley, bratty children playing in the street, the most recent couple he had joined together in holy matrimony. Gordon picked up the phone and heard Gun's question, then he sputtered through his gums, snapped his teeth into his mouth, and proceeded to carry on, congratulatory. Gun's pretty daughter and that nice Hedman boy. Gun hung up on him.

A fresh box of baseballs had arrived yesterday from the store in Minneapolis, the first of a dozen sporting goods stores Gun had purchased after retiring. He went into his bedroom, fished out the box from under the bed, grabbed his bat from behind the bedroom door and went outside to load the machine.

Chapter 10

The hearing next day was held in the upper-level dining hall of the Muskie Lounge, a plush green room used on occasions when the persuasion of comfort was needed. It held about 150 with all folding chairs in use, and at a quarter to twelve the room was noisy with people talking at each other over complimentary drinks. A hush fell as Gun walked in.

Hedman was leaning against the wall, pre-speech drink in hand, three men in pastel suits surrounding him, above their heads a mammoth, wall-mounted muskellunge, treble-hooked Rapala hanging from its angry mouth. Carol Long had arrived and Gun saw her moving gracefully among the county's overweight stratum of importance, her current target being Harold Amudson, whose small eyes widened now at the silver tape-recorder she lifted. It was the size of a cigarette pack. Amudson was a town gas merchant. Until falling into Hedman's camp, his idea of economic development had been to add another line of Little Debbie bars to his snack rack. Now he'd started wearing knit ties and bored anyone willing to listen with development schemes. There was a county board slot coming open in a year— eight months before anyone cared, Harold was running for it.

"I see you're waiting for me!"

Gun knew the voice. Geoff Hedman, tall, smiling, and standing just within the wide double-entry. He wore a linen sport jacket, crisp Levi's, and a Key West tan. To his right, three ladies in bowling jackets ducked and whispered. "Looking fine," Geoff told them. The women giggled. Geoff walked straight to his father, and for a few moments the two conferred. Then Geoff stepped away and headed toward the men's room. Gun followed him.

Inside, he saw Geoff's tan Armadillos tapping a worried waltz under the door of a stall. Gun looked in the mirror, squinted once to define the crow's feet, washed his hands, and leaned against the sink opposite Geoff's stall. When the door swung open, Gun said, "I want to know one thing."

Geoff stood frozen before the coughing toilet. "Mazy isn't here," he said. "She's at home."

"That wasn't the question." He shut the distance between them and stood in the John door, resting a palm on each side. Geoff had nowhere to go. "I want to know how you forced my daughter to marry you."

Geoff's face looked straight ahead, eyes focused on the line of Gun's T-shirt under his collar. "Force her?" he said. His lips spread into a satisfied smile. "We're in love."

Gun laid his hands on Geoff's shoulders, gripping them as if to squeeze ball from socket, then pushed him down on the toilet seat. "If my daughter isn't treated as if your life depends on her safety," he said, "I won't sit you down on a toilet, I'll cram you inside one."

Geoff didn't answer, and Gun slapped the stall closed on his way out.

Every chair in the room had filled, and he moved to the rear wall and stood there, arms crossed on his chest. The Reverend Samuel Barr was at the podium. "Good friends," said Barr, his voice was low and powerful. "Good friends, I thank you for coming. A word of prayer before we begin." He bowed, shanks of thick hair surrounding a bald red dome. "We thank you, Lord, for the chance to improve the lot you've given us. The chance to work and earn, to give our children bread, develop those resources we have at hand."

The prayer rumbled forth unhindered until finally Barr lifted his head, his eyes meeting Gun's from across the room. "... and for the chance to restore our human dignity, amen," he said.

"Dear God," Gun said.

"And now," said Barr, "I'd like to bring up Lyle Hedman. People have been saying he's got a big surprise to spring. That true, Lyle?"

Hedman uncoiled himself from his chair and moved jointlessly to the podium. Gun could see Geoff, recovered from his rest-room trial, blushing near the door.

"Pastor Barr," said Hedman, stooping as he reached the podium, "you have the holiest voice I've ever heard." A few laughs from the crowd, and Gun rolled up on his toes, leaned into the room. Geoff, to Gun's left, had his hands crammed deeply in his pants pockets.

"First, some personal news," Hedman said. "And I have to admit it was a bigger surprise for me than it will be for you. See, my boy Geoff ran out on me over the weekend and came back with a ring on his finger." Hedman unstooped his shoulders and stretched his thin lips in a grin. "The kid went out and eloped, and him a staid thirty years old." He shook his head as if in fond exasperation. "The best part is, he went and found a woman you'll all agree comes from good stock. Mazy Pedersen."

A hundred fifty faces turned to the back of the room. Hedman ran a slick tongue over his parted lips. Gun's eyes stayed on him. Hedman squinted and smiled narrowly. "Gun!" he said. "Gun Pedersen. Damn! Who'd ever thought, right? Guess we never knew how bad our kids had it for each other."

"Guess not," Gun said.

"And Gun, my friend, maybe you'd like to announce the second part of the surprise."

"Floor's all yours," said Gun.

"Thank you," said Hedman. "Ladies and gentlemen, the way has been cleared to build Loon Country Attractions on a suitable site—not that eastside swamp. Provided the referendum goes through, and with the gracious permission of Geoff and Mazy Hedman, the biggest development in the northern half of our beautiful state will go up on the old Pedersen property west of town. Four hundred acres of prime lakefront. Room for the mall, room for hotel accommodations. Time-share condos. Theaters. Restaurants. Jobs. Loon Country Attractions will attract millions of folks each year. Paying customers." He stopped and ran his long fingers through his silver hair. He smiled with his upper teeth at Gun. "Mr. Pedersen," he said. "Why don't you come up and bless the marriage of our children."

Gun turned his head and caught Geoff glaring at him. Geoff was immediately snagged with a fit of coughs.

"Later, then," said Hedman. "A private toast. In the meantime, this is a public hearing—a piece of democracy. Floor's open." Hedman stretched out his long arms.

"What about Larson?" Carol Long spoke from a side table. "Let's hear what Larson thinks." Several voices affirmed the idea, and Hedman smiled at them.

"Of course," he said, and motioned Tig Larson forward. Larson was slow in rising then squeezed between the rows like a baby whale in a tight channel. He was breathing hard. "In the past, of course," Hedman said, "I've known Tig as an eloquent adversary. You all know his record as a conservationist. But now, fortunately for Stony, he's recognized that not all progress leads to Hell.

Commissioner?"

Larson, looking moist in a light summer suit, gained the podium and rested there on his arms. Hedman stepped back and waited. Gun saw Carol scribbling away with her pen.

Larson blew out his cheeks. "There is a time when one confronts certain realities," he said. "And this is such a time. Yes it's important to keep our land and waters healthy. Our lakes are under strain from farmland drainage and acid rain . . ." Gun tried to catch Larson's eye, but the man was watching his hands. "Still, we need the jobs. We need the tourism dollars. Mr. Hedman has promised me that he will protect the water quality at all costs and guard against the destruction of existing lakefront, and . . ." Larson paused. Hedman clasped his hands behind his back, nodding. "And I believe him," Larson finished. "I ask you to vote yes on the referendum."

Gun saw Carol's pen hand pause. Her black eyebrows spiked. Gun turned and walked past Geoff and out of the room.

Chapter 11

At one o'clock a slow breeze from the east was reshaping what had been a pleasant forecast, and people were exiting the Muskie Lounge. Most seemed slightly dazed from Hedman's gift drinks, and willing enough to go to the polls with such generosities in mind. Gun stood in front of the lounge entrance. He was waiting for Larson.

He had to wait a long time.

The first people out were young, hurrying back to untenured positions, checking the creases in their slacks. Then came the sociable threes and fours, holding discussions about the pros of a paved tourist haven in the midst of pines and bright lakes. Gun didn't hear any suggestions about the cons. He stood at the T where the sidewalk met the grass boulevard and listened to the voices die when they passed him. A few said lopsided hellos, looking at Gun's chin when they spoke. He didn't answer. Hedman came out, taller and skinnier than most of his entourage. He was encircled by them, and they moved eagerly around him as if waiting for his autograph, never losing their places. Only Hedman seemed to see Gun as they went by, his beer-colored eyes glistening with confidence.

Larson came out near the end. His tie hung loose on his shoulders, and a damp undershirt showed at the neck.

"You've seen my land before," Gun said.

"Aw, damn," moaned Larson. "Now, suddenly, he cares."

"You've been over every foot of lakeshore. You've been there in the early spring, watching the walleyes spawn."

Larson closed his eyes. "Gun," he said. "I know."

"Explain."

"Can't do it," said Larson. He took a wasted step away from Gun and was halted by a hand against his chest. "Aw, Gun," he said, "it's not your land. It's not even Mazy's land now. It's Hedman's. Everything's Hedman's."

"Tell me something, Tig. How did Hedman know it was all in Mazy's name?"

Larson shrugged, looking down at Gun's hand, still hard against his chest. "How well do you know your lawyer?" he said.

"Not well enough, I guess."

Larson inhaled with effort, pulling air through a pinhole. He said, "Please let me go. I didn't know about his plan. Believe me, I would've told you. Now really, I have to go."

"It's not like you to back down, Tig. Hedman make good on those threats?"

Tig shrugged. "I didn't have any choice. Not this time."

"A person's always got a choice," Gun said.

Tig smiled, eyes flaring. "Of course. And how about Devitz? That poor old bastard have a choice? Did you know he died last night? Hear anybody at the meeting talking about that?"

Gun closed his eyes. "No. No, I didn't." He took his hand away. A sour knot rose in his stomach like yeast. Jeremy Devitz hadn't lasted a month without his land. "I'm sorry."

"I have to go," said Tig.

"Where to?"

"I don't know." His eyes closed, and when they opened they looked flat as the eyes of the dead. "Yes, I do. I'm going to Holliman's Bluff."

"It's a quiet spot," said Gun.

Chapter 12

Nash Sidney's office, the only law office in Stony, occupied what had once been the town's only five-and-dime until Ronnie Truman, the owner, had declared bankruptcy a couple years ago. Now Ronnie operated a car wash south of town and Nash Sidney spent a lot of time alone in his youthful practice on Main Street.

Or had spent time alone. It had been roughly a year since Gun visited him to formalize the transfer of land, house, and personal effects to Mazy's name, and Gun noticed a lot of changes in the formerly sparse office. For starters, when he pushed the door open, there was no dime-store tinkle.

"Hi, Gun," said Nash Sidney. He sat behind a big kidney-shaped desk new enough to smell like varnish. "Miss the bell?"

"You took it down," Gun said. "What would Ronnie say?"

Nash smiled. "He was here last week to talk about a suit. Seems his car wash soaped and waxed the crushed velvet in some lady's Lincoln. Ruined it. She's suing Ronnie because she forgot to roll the window up."

"Glad you still care about client confidentiality."

"He didn't notice the bell," Nash said. "I was disappointed." He rose, tall next to anyone but Gun, and leaned across the desk to shake hands.

Nash Sidney was twenty-eight years old, had graduated from high school a couple years ahead of Mazy and gone to the University of Minnesota on a sports scholarship. Baseball. His fastball and control had been the only happy factors on a sad Stony team for several years, good enough to draw scouts from at least two big-

53

league organizations. Nash chose the university, which made Gun smile, and then law school.

"Business good?" Gun said. He was looking at the kidney-shaped desk, which matched a set of gleaming walnut file cabinets on the back wall.

"Very good," Nash said agreeably. "What summons you to town?"

"Big meeting today. Over at the Muskie. Surprised I didn't see you there."

"The Hedman event, yes. Um, congratulations." Nash sat down again and winced slightly, as though his chair was padded with rocks. "I'd have been there, but the phone wouldn't quit. I have one of those secretaries that only works mornings."

Gun sat down on the hood of Nash's desk. He inhaled through his nose and squinted at a blue-tinted map pinned to Nash's big bulletin board.

"Gun, what's going on?"

"I think I'm finding out. An onerous process, as Jack says." He nodded at the map. "Isn't that a blueprint for Hedman's mall project?"

"Loon Country. Yes."

Gun smiled. "You know, there's something familiar about that shoreline. The way it dips in right there, next to where you've got the talking loon. I wonder where I've seen that before."

Nash was quiet. He took off his glasses and dangled them in his fingers. "Good God. You mean you didn't know? Until today?"

"That Mazy was pulling out with Geoff? Or that my place, her place, is heading for the sewer? And how did you know about any of it, anyway?"

Nash shrugged. "I wouldn't call Loon Country a sewer.

And Mazy could do worse than Geoff Hedman. And I knew about it because I'm Lyle's lawyer. One of them, at least. He's been hinting about the romance, and it wasn't hard to guess the rest. That map there," he poked a thumb at the wall, "is a prospectus. Something Lyle had drawn up, just in case it worked out."

"Just in case," Gun said. "I would have appreciated a call."

"Assumed you knew. You've got a daughter who has a little to do with this, Gun. Don't you and Mazy talk?"

Gun stood up. "Nash, I came in here a year ago and we made a legal transaction. I didn't talk about it. Not to anybody. Now I find out she's joined the Hedman household, and like it or not, she's serving up her inheritence so Lyle can build himself a kingdom. He knew about that land transfer before he should have."

Nash Sidney folded his hands. He looked at Gun as though sizing up a judge, put an appeal in his eyes and said, "I didn't tell him, Gun, if that's what you're thinking."

"That's exactly what I'm thinking."

"Gun, listen. Yes, I handle some private matters for Mr. Hedman. I'm his attorney, for God's sake. I've done some work on his Loon Country thing." Nash's tone now was backstabbed honesty. "But he gets no special favors in this office. And he hasn't asked for any."

Gun stood and rested his right hand on a swooping brass floor lamp that beamed down on Nash's desk. His eyes breezed through the room. "This has turned into a nice little practice for you, Nash. New desk, files, nice carpet. These errands you run for Hedman pay well."

"I have a lot of clients," Nash answered.

"And a whole bushel basket of new ones, once Loon

Country is up and running."

Nash smiled involuntarily and squelched it. "Well, sure. It's a safe guess that new industry in town will bring along some legal holes to plug, and I'll be here to do it. That's my job."

"But that's all you'll get? A few more clients, maybe a full-time secretary? I'd think Hedman would be more grateful than that. Maybe make you his corporate legal advisor, give you a seat on the board." Gun sighed. Being nasty exhausted him.

"Gun, I'm not responsible—" Nash began, but Gun tightened his fingers on the floor lamp's neck and snapped his wrist upward. The brass knuckled back like a garden hose and the beam rested bright on Nash's face. Gun leaned down at the blinking lawyer.

"Tell the truth." he said. "It's easier in the long run."

Nash closed his eyes against the light and ran a handful of fingers through his hair. Gun felt the confession working its way free. He waited.

Nash said, "Might've let it slip, I guess." He kept his eyes closed, as if the words might look worse out in the light.

Gun straightened and walked to the door. Nash sat still under the brass lamp. Gun started to leave the office but was stopped by a thought and leaned back in. "Nash. Why didn't you stick with baseball?"

The lawyer's eyes opened. They were watery as a child's. "I didn't have a curve, Gun. You remember."

"That's right." Gun shrugged. "Well, you've got a beauty now."

Chapter 13

He drove out to the Devitz place after leaving Nash Sidney's office, but Bowser wasn't home. Gun knew where to find him.

Harrelson's Scrub was a 360-acre piece of land that had gone unlived on since the early 1950s. That was when Margie Harrelson, as Gun had heard it, had finally killed herself with the pure mean hard work of farming land meant to remain untilled. Margie left the land to the county when she died. Her son didn't want it.

Gun slowed the old Ford and turned onto the township gravel that ran along the south border of the Scrub. Margie's house was as dead as she was, taken back by rampant willows. Gun stopped the truck and stepped out.

It was colder than it should have been. A gray north wind blew moody clouds over the Scrub, clouds white and the color of ashes. The willows and a few malnourished oaks bent toward Gun in the wind, and the brushy trees beneath them quivered. Gun's hair, white mixed with what was left of blond, flattened against his forehead. There was no open space on the Scrub that he could see, no sign that this land had ever been cleared for the plow, and there was no sign of Bowser. Gun reached back behind the seat of the Ford and pulled out a shirt of nappy brown wool.

Walking was difficult in the Scrub, but the wind was cut. Gun pushed his way through brush and grass that reached to his waist, and ducked his head from branch slaps. Down at his feet something that felt like barbed wire caught and ripped at his ankle. Gun reached down through thick growth and pulled up a reaching bramble.

There was blood on the spines. "Shit," he said, then heard through the tangle of woods and weeds the sound of bursting glass.

"Bowser," Gun said, not loud because the sound of glass had been very close.

"Present," said Bowser's voice. There was crunching in the brush and hard breathing, and then the Scrub parted and Bowser appeared. He was firm and fat, bearded and drunk. There was a mostly empty bottle in his left hand and a homemade slingshot in his right. "Happy day," he said.

"You're here." Gun sighed. His ankle smarted and he could feel his shoe absorbing blood. Bowser waved his bottle in invitation and Gun went with him through the thicket.

Bowser had set up a dark green ice-fishing shack near an old stock pond in the middle of the Scrub. The pond was brown, even in May. Bowser slapped the side of the fish house with the slingshot. "Built this lady in 'sixty-seven," he said. "With the old man. He by-God knew how to put things together." Bowser opened the plywood door and slammed it shut. "All these years and still as solid as earth. It's my goddamned home now and I'm glad of it."

"You still own the home place. Why aren't you there?"

"I don't own nothing." Bowser leaned back with the bottle and swallowed with his eyes shut. "The old man thought Hedman was doing him a favor, leaving us half an acre and the house. Shit."

Gun looked around at the Scrub. "Might be better than living out here."

"You don't believe that," said Bowser.

"I just heard about your dad," Gun said. "I'm sorry."

Bowser's eyes went to Gun's wounded ankle. "Hurt

yourself," he said. He lifted the bottle toward Gun. "Medicine."

"Thanks." The bourbon was cheap and scraped a little on the way down, but the day was cool and Gun welcomed it. He sat down on an upturned five-gallon pail and looked at the ankle. The bramble had snagged him just above the shoe, drilled a neat hole in the flesh between the bone and forward tendon. The hole was deep and clean. He crossed the ankle over his good leg to keep it high, stop the bleeding.

Bowser had opened the fish house again and was sitting down in the narrow doorway. His big thighs were squeezed by the doorframe, and he leaned forward to give his shoulders room.

"Mr. Pedersen, say, have another and pass it on back."

Gun tilted another mouthful of bourbon. There was a splash of liquor still left in the bottle. He tossed it to Bowser.

"Ummm," said Bowser. He finished the bourbon and poked his little finger into the bottleneck. With strain he stood from the doorway and walked, the bottle swinging on his pinky, to a straight thin sapling not six feet tall. He slid the bottle neck down over the tip, and its weight bent the little tree south, with the wind. "For later," he said.

Gun didn't ask.

"So you're here out of kindness?" Bowser said it without sarcasm. "You're sorry about the old man, and maybe feeling bad after kicking my ass the other day?"

Gun smiled. Bowser had faults but possessed the gift of truthful utterance. "Sorry about your dad, yes. Sorry he died without getting your land back from Lyle Hedman."

"People don't get things back from Lyle Hedman."

"Could be you'll be the first. You've heard about the

change in plans? For the Loon Mall?"

"Sure." Bowser didn't seem interested. "He nailed my hind end, then he nailed yours. I felt bad, hearing about it."

"Well. Old Lyle's not going to need your place now."

"You're thinking I should take the money that skinny piece of dog shit gave my old man, go on over to the Hedman place and try and buy it all back."

"You could give it a shot." Gun reached for the shoe he'd taken off. "Worst thing Hedman can do is say no. Or jack up the price."

Bowser put his chin down into his neck and snorted, raking his throat for phlegm. He found some and sent it out into the Scrub. Then he turned and went around the corner of the fish house.

When he came back he was carrying a green cooler. It matched the paint on the fish house. Bowser opened the cooler and brought up a sealed bottle of bourbon. He peered through it at the sky for an instant before twisting off the cap and sampling.

"You know," Bowser said, "I don't think I want that land back."

Gun finished tying his shoe. He stood up. The ankle was stiff but held him upright.

"I think Hedman can keep it and use it or not use it, may he land with a bump in Hell," Bowser said. He put the bottle down in the grass and withdrew the slingshot from his back pocket.

Gun waited. The swallows of bourbon were gone from his blood and the wind was stiff and chill.

"Because," Bowser said, searching at his feet for a stone and finding one, "if that bastard puts up his goddamn mall, on your land or mine, no matter, you're not going to see my great white butt anywhere within fifty miles of it. I'll go north, or I'll go west like my old man. But you won't see me here." Bowser had the stone fitted now and pointed the slingshot almost without looking. He pointed it at the bottle hanging at the tip of the swaying sapling. He pulled the stone almost all the way back to where the black whiskers began on his cheek, and then he let it go. It flew with a bulletlike trajectory, passed through the waistcoat of the dapper gentleman on the bourbon label and dropped pieces of bottle into the grass. The sapling sprang upward, pointing to heaven.

Bowser tossed the slingshot onto the cooler and looked at Gun.

"That's the bareass truth," he said.

Chapter 14

The drive home was cool and whippy with the windows down. Gun could see a mountain range of sea-colored clouds in the rearview mirror of the old F-150. The clouds were diagonally split by a silver shaft where the mirror was cracked. During hunting season of '73, when the truck was two years old, Gun's 30-06 Springfield had rocked out of its back-window saddle on a bad pothole. It bounced forth unloaded, gave Gun a brief crack on the skull, and spun its smooth trigger guard into the mirror. Gun hadn't fixed it since then, and had never again put a firearm into the rack. Now he slid them under the seat.

A mile west of Stony on old County 70 Gun shifted down and turned right on the lake road. He followed it through trees that leaned in to cover the sky: tall black-bruised birches, second generation pines from cones tromped on by waves of loggers, slender aspens brush-stroking in the light wind. Little rips and tears of sky between leaves were blue and getting bluer, the color swelling with humidity the way Minnesota afternoons do before a night rain. Gun slowed the truck and smelled the air like a hound.

Home was left off the township road and three quarters of a mile down a double-rutted truck trail. Weeds exploded from between the ruts, giving the trail a wild look Gun liked. Tourists didn't drive in to ask directions.

***

He had left the right rear burner of the gas stove on. The kitchen was warm and smelled like a winter evening, and mixed with the rising humidity, it was uncomfortable. Gun put out the flame and slid up all the windows that weren't already open. Then he went to the bedroom to change.

When he reentered the kitchen to make lunch, he was wearing cutoff Levi's white from use and a blue short-sleeve work shirt with the armpits ripped. A year ago Mazy had raided her father's dresser and used the shirt to wax her 1968 MG. Gun, in turn, had raided the trash at six o'clock on a Tuesday morning to recover it before Gurney plowed in with his garbage truck. There were still bruises of pink paint dust on the shirt. Gun had saved it for its ripped armpits. They allowed him to swing a bat freely, or a shovel.

There was little food. Gun opened the dank cabinet under the sink and found some potatoes sending colorless shoots through the holes in the plastic sack. There was Dinty Moore beef stew in the cupboard, several cans of ravioli. Gun opened the fridge and saw a lump of dark cheese in plastic wrap, a carton of eggs, half a gallon of yellow buttermilk. He sat on the kitchen table in his shorts, holding the refrigerator open with a foot.

He tapped the fridge door closed and lifted himself off the table, the backs of his legs sticking to the varnish. The air was thickening. He went to the door and stepped out, bending to feel the untrimmed foxtails that angled out from the foundation. They slipped squealing through his fingers. He ripped out a handful and tossed them up, and they drifted down in the direction of North Dakota. Rain tonight. Gun went back to the fridge and took out the carton of buttermilk and the eggs. He also broke from the freezer a block of ice cubes which he dropped into a gallon jar of tea the color of sunsets. He put the tea by the door.

He poured most of the buttermilk into a blender, cracked in four eggs, frothed it up. He took the pitcher off the blender, retrieved the iced tea, and carried both out of the house and down the hill.

Gun's stone boathouse was a project only a few days old. It would be a replacement for an earlier one, a slabwood structure he had built to defend his open Alumacraft from storms and Stony Lake breakers. Its performance had been perfect for a decade until this spring when a tight nor'easter had come riding over Stony Lake like a chariot, blowing the tops of the waves into grapeshot spray. Gun had stood at the window and watched. It took the wind and waves three minutes to put the boathouse asunder, and when the air was free of slabwood, he'd gone out and yanked the dented boat up into the outfield grass.

Now there was nothing on the lakefront but a clean square hole. Gun had sandbagged a small dry area where the hole opened out onto the shore, had spaded out and poured eighteen-inch footings. The old boathouse hadn't had the benefit of a solid anchor. This time he would build on rock. Not for himself—he wasn't going to be here. Probably not for anybody. But it made him feel useful, defiant. And it was a good habit: finish what you start.

A hump of spray-cleaned lake stones lay on the grass next to the hole—enough, Gun figured, for four feet of solid wall on three sides. He went to the shed and retrieved two sacks of ready-mix concrete and a large steel bucket. He poured half the mix into a fifty-five-gallon drum between the footings, then added buckets of water from the lake and stirred and slapped at the gray mud until it was flabby and made noise like the quicksand in old Tarzan movies. As he moved the trowel over the footings, laying a base for the bottom tier of stones, Gun felt the first stiffening of the small east breeze.

She's at home, waiting for me. So said Geoff, and the statement wouldn't leave his mind. Something was off. Gun wanted to believe it was Geoff, who'd never shown more character than the pampered fool he appeared, just doing his old man's coercive bidding. But there was another possibility, and Gun had to admit there was precedent for it: maybe, once again, he'd managed to read his daughter exactly wrong.

He picked up one of the stones from the pile, hefted it to his shoulder, took three quick steps toward the water and heaved. The rock came down twenty yards out with a detonating splash that did nothing to quell his unease.

After setting four layers of lakestone, Gun climbed out, reached for the buttermilk mixture and tilted it up. It cooled and slightly sickened him. He traded the pitcher for the tea, watery now. The cold jar balanced with a wholesome weight in Gun's palm. The sky was darkening. Half the pile of rocks was still on the ground.

Back in the hole, Gun worked fast, troweling mud, eyeing from the pile the right stone to fit each circumstance. Mazy had helped him build the first boathouse when she was fifteen, handing him nails to put between his teeth. Today she had not even been at the meeting where it was announced that her land would soon be dead and interred beneath cement and glass and tourists.

The rock pile disappeared a quarter of an hour before dark. It was enough time for Gun to take a mouthful of warm egg buttermilk, spit it away, swim once out to the walleye bed to rinse away the grit, and go inside to bed.

Chapter 15

Tuesday came up light blue and warm, the blurring humidity washed out of the sky by what Gun estimated had been a two-inch downpour overnight. The rain had muddied the walls and floor of Gun's boathouse, but hadn't damaged the mortar work. The gray cement had set up fast, and now held trails of silt and dirt between the rocks where the water had run. No more masonry for the present.

The grass and weeds soaked Gun's tennis shoes as he walked to the infield. The pitching machine, tarped against the rain, had come through the storm honorably. With his free hand Gun undid the twine holding the tarp and pulled it into a heap behind the mound.

The machine undraped, wheels spinning, tripod legs quivering, a dozen baseballs in the hopper, Gun waited patiently at home. On mornings this light he sometimes smote baseballs so far his eyes lost them in the general whiteness of the sky. More than thirty years ago he'd done the same thing in front of a major-league scout, who told him frequent repetitions would earn him a living. It turned out that way.

Now the machine ticked and trembled, and a ball was seized and spun toward home at big-league velocity. Gun swung and made slight contact, launching the ball nearly straight up. He counted a hang time of eight before the ball came down just back of the machine. The arm snapped again, and this time Gun sent a hard grass burner through the hole between third and short. It sent up a thin cloud of spray that rainbowed briefly in the sunshine. Gun shook his head and twisted the bat in his hands. He jabbed his toe at the ground. Inhaled, kept his lungs full. The next pitch came in chest high, and the club end of the Hillerich and Bradsby met it hard, a fraction of an inch below center. The ball rose outward, lakebound. He tried to follow its course but the white morning air had sunspots. It struck the lake with a distant *hock*.

"I saw Jim Rice do that at Fenway once," said Carol Long. She was standing in the weeds behind Gun and to the left. In the third-base dugout.

"Sweet heaven," Gun said. "You're early, game doesn't start till one."

"I always come for batting practice." Carol stepped out of the tall gras. She wore green spring walking shorts. "Go ahead," she said. "Hit a few more."

"I'll hit later," he said. The machine clicked and fired, and he held out the bat in an impromptu one-hand bunt. "Sometimes they get lost in the grass," he explained.

"Or the lake," said Carol.

Gun walked to the pitching machine and killed it just before it kicked into another cycle. He turned to Carol, who was standing now in the region of the coach's box. Her arms were crossed. Gun smiled. One season crossed arms had been a signal to steal. The next year it meant look out for the pickoff. "I'm glad to see you," he said. "Should I be?"

She waved a legal-sized notebook. "I'm working on a story . . ."

"Ah."

Carol uncrossed her arms and started toward him. "I've lived in Stony nearly a month and never seen the much-bespoken Gun Pedersen land," she said. "Or not much of it."

"You want to find out exactly what it is Hedman's trying to trash."

Carol had reached him at the pitching machine. There were a few thin leaves of pale wet grass sticking to her ankles, just above the sandals.

"I didn't know about it myself until the day before yesterday," Gun said. "Or know for sure."

Her green shorts had abstract white designs. On top she wore a loose white cotton pullover with wrinkles at the shoulders.

"I've decided not to let them do it," said Gun. It was a statement that he hadn't known was true until he spoke.

Carol's face was direct and open. The fall of her bangs across her forehead stirred in the breeze. Her perfume was something of island origin, and near enough to feel.

"Want to look around?"

"Yes."

The four hundred acres made for a long morning's walk. He showed her the coastal hollows that changed shape with each spring's gouging ice-melt, a sudden twenty-acre clearing where the trees fell off to willowy shrubs and then to rushes, the clear-running stream that left Stony Lake and headed west. Finally they climbed a small rise at Gun's northern boundary. Underfoot was a cushion of needles and above rose some of the last virgin pines in the logbelt.

"They were here," Gun said, staring up, "before anything."

"Like the redwoods in California." Carol tilted her head back. "What kept the loggers from cutting them?" she asked.

He kept his eyes on the treetops. "I guess when the first loggers got here there were still some Indian legends around. One of them was about an Ojibwe chief named Shadow Horse. He was a giant apparently. Plus fast and smart. He died fighting for his people, and they buried him up here."

"So the loggers stayed away? I'm surprised."

"Legend says that when Shadow Horse's grave is violated, he'll come alive again, madder than hell. Maybe the loggers didn't want to chance it."

Carol said, "I thought the loggers had Paul Bunyan on their side."

"It's just a guess, but I think Paul Bunyan would have walked on tiptoe to keep from waking Shadow Horse."

"And Lyle Hedman?" said Carol.

Gun turned to look at her. The sun was touching her black bangs, highlighting the few silver strands. A trace of perspiration sparkled on her cheekbones. "What do you think?" he said.

Carol waited to answer until Gun took the first step back toward home. Then she said, "I think Lyle Hedman should step carefully. Old legends have a way of coming back."

***

"All right, journalist, what have you got?" Gun said. They were sitting on Gun's log porch holding stoneware mugs of iced tea.

Carol frowned and leaned back in the rough-hewn chair. "I'm having a hard time finding the handle, if you want to know the truth, Gun," she said. "I think it's about time you leveled with me, told me what your gut says." Carol took a sip of tea without removing her eyes from Gun's face. "Did she want to marry the guy or not?"

Gun laughed and looked away. "The more I think, the more I don't know. If I knew she was in some kind of trouble I wouldn't be sitting here—but at this point what can I do?" He stabbed a finger into the palm of his hand. "I've got to find a reason, one good reason. Something that'll tell me she needs help. I don't have that."

Carol nodded.

Gun leaned toward her. "What do you think? You're a friend—she probably talks to you more than she does me."

"She mentioned Geoff a few times. Told me about that night in the woods, the prank he and his friends pulled. She said how much she hated him."

"Bastard."

"But she also said—about a week ago, after she'd started the story—how she was beginning to understand him. How the two of them had things in common. Powerful fathers, the fear of not living up to expectations, you know. She said she was almost getting fond of Geoff, much as she hated to admit it."

Gun snorted and waved off her words.

"I'm just telling you what she said."

"I wasn't made for waiting around," Gun said.

"There was something. Mazy mentioned it before I left for Minneapolis last week. She didn't know if it was important, but it had her stumped."

Gun waited.

"Loon Country's a four-hundred-million-dollar project, right?" said Carol. "And supposedly all the money's lined up: the local efforts are on track, bond sales, pull tabs, stuff like that. And the heavy hitters are committed. Tynex in Minneapolis for a hundred mil, Diamond Inns, all of those you've heard about. But here's the thing. Mazy said she was looking through Hedman's projections and it added up to about three hundred million, a hundred short. She showed her figuring to Lyle and he just laughed and pointed to a name on the list of investors. 'The balance is right here,' he told her."

"Who was it?" said Gun.

"I don't remember. I'd never heard the name before."

"You don't remember anything?"

"I want to say it sounded African. A foreign word, I think."

Gun spent the next five minutes trying to jog Carol's memory, but nothing clicked. Then she looked at her watch and said she needed to get going, there were interviews to do before press time. "Wait a minute, though," she said suddenly. "Tig Larson."

"What?"

"I didn't tell you. Apparently he never went home after the hearing yesterday."

"Probably headed for Minneapolis," said Gun. "He has friends there."

"I don't know. There was a county board meeting last night. Larson doesn't usually miss those—and he wasn't there. And Chief Bunn was out looking this morning. Stopped by the paper to see if I'd seen him."

"Bunn? What did Larson do?"

"Nothing. I guess Larson's garage was empty and the door was open and the storm last night rolled the neighbor's trash can in next to the Lawn Boy. It spilled all over. Bunn just thought it was strange that Larson wouldn't be there, cleaning stuff up."

Gun frowned.

"I saw you talking to him after the meeting," Carol said. "What did he seem like?"

"Tired, frustrated. Depressed and a little drunk. And scared, maybe."

"He didn't mention if he was leaving town?"

"Nope. He said something about Holliman's Bluff, like he might do some fishing."

"Fishing?" Carol looked off toward the water. "Maybe he thought he owed it to himself after that performance at the lodge." She lifted the stoneware mug but stopped before touching it to her lips. Gun was on his feet and his face was gray.

"We'll take the truck," he said.

They were quiet on the ride. Holliman's Bluff was thirteen miles away, a dramatic chunk of upthrust rock that rose from the lake to a height of forty feet. There was a sign at the crest where the highway bent away from the lake: HOLLIMAN'S BLUFF—SCENIC PARKING. There was room for half a dozen cars. On summer nights boys in family rods brought their girls to the bluff, while below them men in silver and red Lund boats fished for walleyes on the shelf. The sheer rock cliff went straight down about ten feet into the water, then stuck out its shelf like a knee for several yards and dove again to lake bottom and a final depth of a hundred feet.

No one was parked at the bluff now, and no boats were working the shelf. Gun and Carol walked to the edge and looked over.

"What exactly are we doing here?" said Carol.

"I hope to God we're wasting our time," said Gun. He shaded his eyes with the flat of his hands, squinting down into the water.

"What do you see?" said Carol.

"Nothing."

"What are you looking for?"

"A county commissioner."

"Right. God."

Gun glared at the water for another two minutes. Then he walked back to the truck and stood eyeing the parking area in front of the bluff.

"You're looking for tire tracks," said Carol.

"Like these." Gun pointed at a depression in the grass. "Or not. I'm no expert, and the rain's wrecked everything anyway. Maybe I'm inventing it."

Carol couldn't see the tracks. Gun said, "I'm going in." He pulled off his shoes and T-shirt, stepped to the edge of the bluff, and dove.

Chapter 16

Stony Lake in May was clear and arctic, the algae not yet in bloom. Two months ago a car driven over Holliman's Bluff would have crashed and burned on thirty inches of pack ice. Now Gun's eyes stung with cold as he opened them underwater.

He found nothing on his first dive. The spring runoff had been high this year, and the pull down to the shelf felt farther than ten feet. He maintained a depth of about six, his head humming from the pressure, and kicked slowly, following the shelf off to the left. He surfaced, blowing, thirty yards farther along the bluff from where Carol stood.

"Anything?" yelled Carol.

Gun shook his head, panting. He waved numb limbs, treading water, then went down again.

Tig Larson sat in his gray Buick Century another twenty yards along. The Buick was parked on the shelf with the right wheels hanging off the edge so it tilted like a car driven up on a curb. Larson was floating in the confines of a seat belt and shoulder strap, only lightly touching the seat. His heavy face looked straight up through the sunroof of the Buick, toward sunlight ten feet above. Gun pushed away from the car and let himself rise to the surface.

"He's here," he called to Carol, who'd followed his course along the top of the bluff.

"God, oh." Her hands were clamped into fists. She jammed them in her pockets.

"I think I'd better bring him up." Gun shook his head to throw the water from his eyes, pulled in a heavy lungful of air and bobbed under.

He reached the Buick again and opened the door. It swung in slow motion, and he reached in and unclipped the seat belt. Larson was stiff in his sitting position, and his knees whacked against the steering wheel when Gun snagged his collar and tried pulling him out. The Buick rocked softly on the edge of the shelf, and he realized the need for care. If the car went over the side carrying Larson, it would take equipment and divers to bring Larson up. Not that it mattered too much. With the blood bumping in his arteries, he reached forward and straightened Larson's legs at the knees.

The commissioner's hands floated an inch above his lap, and Gun saw and barely registered that several of his fingers were missing, cleanly nipped at the second joints. The turtles had already been here. Gun took Larson by the waving hair and leaned him out the door. When Larson was clear, Gun shoved him skyward. Larson drifted up through twilight, legs straight out front, face turned up. He looked like a child sitting on the floor, staring at the ceiling. Gun pushed off from the shelf and beat Larson to the surface.

"Couldn't you get him?" Carol said, almost before Gun's head pushed up into the waves. A ruffling breeze was coming from the northwest.

Gun was too busy refilling to talk. He motioned with his head at a spot a few feet to his left. Larson was unhurriedly surfacing there.

"Oh no," said Carol.

"I'm going to look through his car," said Gun, breathing hard. "Then I'll tow him in."

"I'll take your truck," Carol said, "get the police."

Gun shook his head, swam a tired stroke to Larson and set off for a shallow slope of shore with the county commissioner riding behind.

The Stony authorities had not been confronted with a body for over two years, not since the last time Funny Harbon Starling and his buddy Jerry had gone sprinting over thin ice in Harbon's Power Wagon. It was something the two of them had done every November for fourteen years, proving their manhood. Finally the ice opened and swallowed them, burping up the bodies in the spring storm wash. Sheriff Bakke had turned white at the scene and threatened to turn in his badge.

Bakke was at the bluff now along with two cops, and blinking rapidly at Larson. "Ah, damn it, Tig. When's the last time either of you saw him?"

"Yesterday," Gun said. "At the public meeting. Like you and most of the town."

"Carol?"

"Same."

"How'd you happen to find him?"

"I tried to talk to him, after the meeting. He mentioned the bluff. I thought he meant to go fishing."

Carol, at his side, was rubbing him down with his shirt.

Bakke sighed. "He was in his car?" he said.

"Yeah."

"In a seat belt, you said."

"One of those habits it's hard to break."

"We'll call you," said Bakke. He turned and walked to the two policemen, who were gesturing over the body. "I don't know," he said to them. "Law enforcement. Shit."

"I need to get dry," Gun said to Carol. The northwest wind was steady and the waves were getting higher and farther apart. Carol held out his keys. "You drive," he said.

At home Gun put on dry jeans and a chamois shirt

while Carol poked through a *Baseball Abstract* on the kitchen table.

"Do you need to get back to the paper?" Gun asked her, returning to the kitchen.

"Deadline's eleven o'clock tonight," Carol said. She smiled. "I'd better get back by ten."

"Let's take a drive, then."

"Where to?"

Gun held up a small triangular wad of paper. It was wet and clumped together, but the words printed on it were legible. He tossed it on the table.

"The Back Forty." Carol looked up. "A bar napkin? I never heard of it."

"I found it on Larson when you drove up to Podolske's to call the cops."

"God. You searched the body. Shouldn't you have given them the napkin?"

"Given it to Bakke?" Gun shrugged. "He wouldn't have done anything with it."

"What's there to do? It's a bar napkin."

Gun shrugged again. "Don't know. Are we going for a drive?"

"Will we talk on the way?"

"If you like."

"Let's take my car then," said Carol.

When they were in the car, both of Carol's hands at the bottom of the plastic steering wheel, she said, "What's with the Back Forty?" The front seat of the Horizon was pushed back to its outer limit. Gun's knees were against the dash. The Back Forty was thirty miles to the south.

"It has a reputation," Gun said.

"What sort?"

"It's a gay bar, Carol."

"So?" she said. Then three miles later: "Why are we following Larson's backtrail?"

"I can only think of one reason right now," said Gun. "Mazy."

"I'm missing a link somewhere."

"Hedman. What if he was threatening to expose Tig?"

Carol made a so-what sound with her lips. "Gun, that's ridiculous. Who would care?"

Gun said, "You've got to remember, Larson was first elected commissioner twenty years ago. Just a kid out of grad school. Folks were proud of him. He had one of those green ecology stickers on the back of his Beetle. Caught the guy from the old Shell station dumping used oil in the Woman River. It made Tig a folk hero. And in Stony, folk heroes weren't gay. Not then."

"But it hasn't been a big secret, has it? For a long time?"

"Look," said Gun, "in a small town it's one thing for everyone to think they know something. It's another altogether to shout it from the housetops."

"What's the connection to Mazy?"

"Hedman might be a swindler and a blackmailer," Gun said, "and maybe much worse. And he has Mazy. I think that's connection enough."

Carol was silent. Gun said, "I should just go in. Go in and get her out."

"You haven't given her a chance," said Carol. "She hasn't asked for help."

"Has she been able to?" Gun shifted his knees and the red plastic dash bent and creaked.

The Horizon, engine racing at fifty miles an hour, passed a homemade sign. THE BACK FORTY, it said. SEVEN MILES AND TO YOUR RIGHT. SEE YOU THERE.

Chapter 17

The place had the tucked-under look of a basement house or a 1950s bomb shelter. It sat squarely next to the county blacktop, with a short gravel drive and a ten-car lot. A sign on the door said BACK FORTY LOUNGE.

Gun uncoiled himself from the Horizon. He could feel a rubbing in his kneecaps as he stood up straight.

"I think we got here too soon," said Carol. "No one's here."

Gun walked slowly to the edge of the lot and peeked around the building. He saw a banged-up brown dumpster under a cloud of flies, and behind it an early seventies yellow Toyota Corolla. "It's business hours," he called to Carol.

Eyebrows high, Carol pushed at the door. It swung open. The place seemed larger on the inside, with the low-hanging lamps turned down to a glow.

"Are you sure there's someone here?" Carol spoke in a whisper.

"Should be," said Gun. His voice was at normal volume but seemed big in the dark. "There's a car out back. The door was open." He walked ahead of her, skirting the barely-lit chairs and tables.

"Ouch," said Carol. "Shinned a chair. How can you see in here?"

A light clicked on immediately to their right. In its beam they saw a young man in a shiny white buttondown shirt. He was something over six feet and had a thick black mustache and thin black eyebrows. He was standing behind a bar.

"Just opening up," he said in a tentative voice. "Nobody's usually here so early. What can I get you?"

"A little help, if you can," Gun said. "You know a guy named Tig Larson? County commissioner, lives in Stony."

The barkeeper looked at Gun, then cautiously at Carol and back at Gun. "I know who Larson is." he said.

"We need to know who he hung out with in here. And how recently."

"Seriously? Something happen to him?"

"He drove into Stony Lake off a cliff," said Carol.

"Oh, no."

"Who did he know here?" said Gun.

The bartender looked away. He said, "Man, I'm sorry to hear this. But I don't know you guys. You understand? Discretion means my job."

"I'm Gunsten. This is Carol." Gun leaned forward on the bar. "We knew Tig and liked him. Don't think of this as indiscretion—think of it as obligation."

"Actually, Mr. Larson wasn't here very often."

The bartender was quiet. He started to speak, stopped, and went ahead. "A guy named Rutherford, Dan Rutherford. Sort of a new face. Don't think I ever saw him before, say, a month ago. He was at some resort, I think."

"Was Rutherford here often?" said Carol.

"Only with Larson. Hell, I think they met here. The Friar introduced them."

"The Friar?"

"Yeah, the Friar—older guy, circle of hair on top. Like Friar Tuck, right? I don't know his name. Comes in every few months. He brought Rutherford in, sat him down next to Larson."

Gun sat down on the bar stool. "Rutherford," he said. "Which resort?"

"God, you think Rutherford did something to off Larson?"

"No. Which resort?"

The bartender leaned back against a rack of whiskey. He closed his eyes. "The Broken Rock," he said. "I think the Broken Rock, I heard the name once or twice."

"Thank you," said Carol.

"Got a phone I can use?" Gun asked.

The bartender pointed.

Gun went over and dialed information, then rang the Broken Rock where a young child's voice came on the line. "My dad's not here now."

"When is he coming back? Later tonight?"

"He's here in the morning," said the child.

"Okay, thanks," Gun said.

Chapter 18

By the time they entered Stony the sky was low and dense, the air sharp with the smell of rain. At the east edge of town he turned into the driveway of Peaceful Haven, the resort where Carol was renting a small cabin, number four, which sat on a rock ledge twenty feet above the lake. It was painted light green, same as the other buildings, and a big stone chimney covered one end. Gun braked to a stop and let the engine idle. Carol didn't open her door. "We're going to get some weather tonight," Gun said. "You might want to collect enough dry wood for a couple days, in case this front decides to hang around."

"I don't know how to use the fireplace. There's a little gas burner in my bedroom, and I turn that on if I need to." She tapped her lips with an index finger.

"I'll find some dry wood. Won't take long to get a little flame going."

Carol looked at him. "All right, then. You make the fire, and I'll make supper. How's that?"

"Deal."

In fifteen minutes he had enough dry wood for a week of evening warm-up fires: fast-burning birch, some half-rotted branches of pine, and a few whitened lengths of driftwood, delicately curved and smooth as skin. From the neat stack he made on the screened-in porch he took a high armful of wood and carried it inside. The kitchen was cabbage-colored—and smelled like cabbage too, Gun noticed. He walked into the compact living room, paneled with a darkly stained particle board, and lowered his load onto the brick hearth.

"Hope you like cabbage," Carol said from the kitchen.

"What's it belong to?"

"New England boiled dinner."

"Great," he said, though it wasn't what he expected, not from a long-time islander. Seafood maybe, or something Chinese, Italian. But boiled cabbage and corned beef? He turned from building a pyramid of sticks on the iron rack. Carol was setting the table, facing away. The backs of her legs looked smooth and tan.

When the food was ready, they moved the kitchen table into the living room, and there, with the fire throwing shadows against the wall, they ate in silence. He wanted to say something about how nice this was, how for the first time in his life he was enjoying the taste of cabbage, even the smell of it, God help him. But he was also thinking of Mazy, and how he wasn't doing her a lot of good here.

From the west came the first rumblings of a storm and from the lake the sad cry of a loon, an airy high-low wailing. Carol said, "I understand how you're feeling, Gun. I'm a parent too. Here, help me"—she stood and took hold of one end of the table. "Let's get it back in place then sit by the fire awhile. We've earned it, haven't we?"

He helped her with the table, then knelt at the hearth. A chunk of smoldering pine had fallen from the iron rack.

"Time you learned about me," Carol said. "I already know about you—and not just from that godawful biography that came out when you retired."

"Unauthorized."

"Right. I got the inside story from your daughter."

"Oh, boy."

She fell into one of the stuffed chairs and crossed her ankles on a wooden footstool at Gun's side. He laid a few splintered pieces of birch onto the red and white coals, leaned down and blew a steady stream until a flame began to flash up from the coals and lick at the new wood.

"Aren't you going to sit?" Carol said.

"In a second."

"I'll start with the inauspicious beginnings. Livingston, Montana, rancher's daughter, sister of four brothers, model child until the age of sixteen." She tapped her toes together. Her feet were nearly touching Gun's elbow. He reached over and took one in his hand.

"Fire feels good," Carol said. "Hand, too."

"So. Sixteen."

"I decided Montana was no place for a woman with ambition," Carol said. "Didn't want to end up a rancher's wife. So I talked my parents into letting me spend my last year of high school in California with an aunt."

Gun gave her foot a squeeze and stood from his crouch, moved to the chair beside her. The fire was snapping and breathing, spitting orange sparks the chimney draft sucked away. The thunder was getting closer, and now a jarring crack shook the cabin. At the same instant a shot of lightning exploded at the living room window, and for a moment everything was as bright as noon. Then it was darker than before, and quieter, until the first large drops struck the roof.

Gun waited for Carol to go on, watched her profile in the fire's uneven light.

"The next few years, I don't know how they went by so fast. Bad decisions are great for speeding up your life. I graduated from high school in San Diego, started college there, got through the first year. And then along came this guy who seemed to know everybody. Big name-dropper—actors, producers, media people. Asked me to go to Hawaii with him. Told me if I did, I'd be a model in six months. I went. In six months he was gone and I was looking for a job. Too proud to go home, of course. I started at the *Honolulu Advertiser*, ground floor, writing obits. They're habit-forming, you know, I still write them. This afternoon, for instance—you're bringing Tig up from his car, I'm writing the poor guy's eulogy in my head."

"So the guy left you, and you got a job."

"Right. That was Stan the First—man of many promises. Next I met Stan the Second, who was just the opposite. Silent strength and all that. Out of gratitude for his quiet ways, I married him." Carol stopped. The rain on the roof was finally letting up.

"And you had a child."

She nodded. "Michael. He's twenty now, studying in California. You'd like him."

"I bet I would," Gun said. "What happened to Stan number two?"

"He found his dream job and his dream girl. When I married him, he was a student at the University of Hawaii, studying to be a park ranger. After Michael was born, Stan graduated and took a job in Redwood National Forest. I waited in Hawaii while he went on ahead—but instead of getting the call telling me to pack up the baby and join him, I got the one asking for a divorce. We were together a year."

The rain had stopped and the rumbling had moved off to the east. The wood in the fireplace had turned to gray ash.

"And for the last two decades I've been learning journalism and saving to buy my own paper. I'll spare you the play-by-play."

"Another time," Gun said.

Neither spoke for a while. The skies quieted and the rain stopped. Carol laughed softly. "You were really something to watch today, you know that? Diving off the cliff into the water, and bringing up Larson from that car?" She bit at her emerald ring. "Something bothers me, though. I don't know how to put it. It was almost like you were . . . enjoying yourself. Am I wrong?"

Gun pushed himself straight in his chair and placed his palms flat on the corduroy-covered arms. He drew a long breath and blew his lungs empty. "Look," he said. "It's been a long hard day."

"Okay," said Carol, nodding. "Does it have to be over?"

He leaned into her and picked up her hand and slowly traced around it with an index finger before replacing it in her lap.

"There'll be another time," she said.

He stood up, then bent and kissed her on the forehead. "I'm glad you said that."

Chapter 19

He drove home with the windows down, the storm-cleared air washing the inside of the truck. He thought of Mazy, about who she was and why. He pushed away the picture of Tig Larson and his nipped-off fingers. And he remembered how Carol had stood on the bluff that afternoon, looking for him in the freezing water, the lake breeze snapping at her hair. Then exhaustion, along with the wind in the cab, emptied his mind and made the trip home as easy as sleep.

There was a solitary letter in his mailbox, one he normally would have thrown away. But tonight the logo of the smiling child hooked something in his brain, made him remember:

The messenger had arrived a week after the World Series—*his* World Series, fifteen RBI, six home-runs, series MVP—and Gun was home alone when the door bell rang. Amanda and Mazy were out buying groceries. The man said his name was Rudy and he had something to deliver from a Mr. Cheeseman. It was hard not to stare at Rudy's face. The left eye was normal, but the right had an iris like a little green sequin awash in the white.

"Who's Cheeseman?" Gun asked.

"Businessman, import-export," Rudy said. He slipped a yellow envelope from the inner pocket of his coat. "Has an interest in baseball, loves the game. Sends you a small gift."

"Can't take it," Gun said, stepping back and starting to swing the door closed. "And I don't know any Cheeseman."

Rudy took a step forward and put a hand on the door. "He won't appreciate my coming back if the delivery hasn't been made." The strange eye sparkled, and Gun believed him. He took the envelope, tore it open, and tilted a check for $35,000 into his hand.

"Can I tell him you said thanks?" said Rudy.

"Tell him I will see him."

"That wouldn't be wise. Just spend and enjoy. You earned it."

It took Gun half the afternoon to find Cheeseman's import basement in downtown Detroit. He got the name of the company off the check—he wished he remembered it now—and looked up the address in the Yellow Pages. It was a moldering brick edifice, and the entrance to Cheeseman's concern was below street level. Something or other LTD, it said on the door. Gun went inside, not knowing what to expect. What he found was like a set from the *African Queen*, banana plants bursting under grow-lights, red and blue parrots preening in miniature palm trees, a family of taxidermied cheetahs at play among the greenery. A tape played a loop of screaming birds and hissing night-bugs. A fat man with a watering can led Gun through a wall of hanging vines, past two stuffed jackals and into an office where Cheeseman was parked behind a large desk talking quietly on the phone. He didn't even bother with a call-you-later, just put the receiver in the cradle when Gun entered. Cheeseman stood, a man about fifty and charging toward coronary, his hard round face showing a small blush of pleasure.

"Friedrich Cheeseman," he said, putting out his hand. "And you, by God, are Gun Pedersen."

Gun shook the hand warily.

"I'm happy you came. I've watched you for years—you're an artist. And those clutch hits last week doubled my net worth in Reno. I'm indebted to you."

"Listen—"

"On the other hand, I'm sorry you're here. Rudy told me I'd see you, and I'm guessing you have my check in your wallet and that you're aching to hand it back to me."

"I have it, yes."

Cheeseman chuckled. "Old Rudy. Got a bitch of an eye problem, but he can judge character." He sat down again and motioned Gun to a leather chair. "The thing is, I reward people who deserve it. Doesn't matter if they did it for me."

Gun put a hand to his shirt pocket.

"Please. You're concerned about dirty money—what a wonderful example for our children. But your check draws from the import section of my business, items gathered from the great continent and sold at a markup. Legitimate business."

"And safaris, do you handle those?" Gun asked on impulse.

"Of course we do," Cheeseman said. Then his eyes went gray, in warning. "Did you know, some African tribes consider it an insult if a man returns a gift. Bad luck, like breaking a mirror. And I doubt that either of us needs bad luck."

Gun stood, leaving the check in his pocket. He opened the door.

"You're one sweet hitter, Gun," Cheeseman said, smiling now. "And I expect we'll see each other again."

"I doubt it," Gun said, and left.

He wondered at first what to do with it. Tear it up? Send it to Cheeseman via mail? Put it in a drawer and forget about it? In the end he sent the whole chunk to a children's fund in Missouri—Mazy had a pen pal there. And since then, he'd heard from Missouri several times a year: Thank you for your past generosity. The letter today was no different, and he crumpled it and hit the wastebasket on the first try, banking it off the fridge.

***

He woke at three A.M. to the sound of an elephant blaring a high-pitched alarm. In his dream he had approached it from behind, rifle in hand, and the animal had turned, red eyes ablaze. Gun sat up in bed and identified the sound: the double-trunked birch outside his window, sawing in the wind. He lay back, shutting his eyes, and at the tricky border between sleep and consciousness found himself standing in a boat on a clear lake and seeing on the sandy bottom a check for $35,000 from Kudu Club, LTD. Higher, in the middle depths, was Lyle Hedman's stuffed elephant, its heavy legs treading water. And higher still, just beneath the lake's surface, the list of Hedman's investors Carol had mentioned. He couldn't make out names.

He lay still and waited for his thumping heart to calm, told himself the connection was unlikely. All the same, it was common knowledge that Lyle and Mrs. Hedman took frequent trips to Reno—Friedrich Cheeseman's stomping ground. And of course there was the fact of Lyle's safari trips and his African curios. How farfetched was it to think that Cheeseman might be an investor in Lyle's project? And if Lyle was mixed up with Cheeseman, how farfetched to think Lyle was being outplayed?

"In the morning I'll find out," Gun said to the darkness. Then he fell back into dreams of zebras and lions, and hyenas laughing.

Chapter 20

Cheeseman's number was unlisted, and no one at Kudu Club's home office in Reno admitted to knowing anything about a development project in Minnesota. One man, a marketing vice-president and the fifth person in Gun's tag-team conversation, said, "Minnesota? Yeah, nice town —stopped there once on my way to Chicago."

Gun hung up and dialed the number again, asked for customer service. A honey-voiced woman named Camille came on the line and Gun told her his name was Lyle Hedman. He complained that the elephant he had shot and had stuffed was getting saggy in the belly. "How long ago?" Camille asked. Gun said he couldn't remember. Ten, twelve years ago maybe. She went to look it up, then came back with the verification Gun needed.

"Yes, nine years ago, Mr. Hedman. And the invoice was signed by Mr. Cheeseman himself. In fact yours was the first elephant taken by one of our clients. May I pass you along to Mr. Anders, who handles these matters?"

"Please," Gun said, and he hung up.

***

The morning sun was bright as he drove along County 13 in the direction of Tornado Lake and the Broken Rock Resort, hoping to learn what he could about the man named Rutherford who might or might not have something to do with poor Tig Larson's unexpected change of mind and untimely death. Lyle Hedman would have to wait until later.

Gun had been thinking about his conversation with the bartender at the Back Forty, but what he recalled hadn't shaken loose any memories. Then, however, he rounded a curve that bordered a reed-filled bay and the sign came into view—BROKEN ROCK RESORT, SINCE 1941, the letters arranged on the logo of a boulder split in two, and that jogged something upstairs. Fourth of July, early eighties, a sultry afternoon in Emersonville, a small town south of Tornado, where Gun had agreed, oddly, to throw out the first pitch in a softball tournament. The man he threw it to, and whose uniform bore the same logo, was proprietor of the Broken Rock—a chatty guy, it turned out, and Gun remembered having to listen to him prattle on for longer than he would have liked.

He parked the old Ford in front of the building marked OFFICE and went inside. Standard fare: low-ceilinged with a bar straight ahead, a game room with pool tables, pinball on one side, tables and booths on the other. Gun stepped up to the bar and bumped the countertop bell with his fist. It took about three seconds for the man to appear from a back room. Same guy—shoulders wide and sloping, large face with whisker shade, small nose.

"Gun Pedersen! Hell yeah!" He stuck out his hand and Gun shook it. "Been a while. Let's see—1983 was the year we played catch, wasn't it? Sit, sit, I'll get you a beer on the house."

Gun took a stool.

The man touched the tips of his fingers against both of Gun's shoulders. "Goddamn," he said. "What'll it be? We got Miller, Pabst, and Mick."

"You pick."

"'You pick.' Love it, love it." He grabbed a glass mug from a nearby stack and drew from the tap, never removing his eyes from Gun's face, then clapped it down on the bar. "There you be."

"Thank you," Gun said. "What's your name again?"

The man looked hurt for a moment, then he brightened. "Slacker, Larry Slacker."

"Yes," Gun said.

Larry drew a beer for himself, pulled up a stool and sat down on his side of the bar. A bead of sweat clung to his short nose. He was grinning. "What brings you out this way—fishin' Tornado? And let me tell you, my people are catching crappies the size of dinner plates without so much as getting their damn boats wet. Hell, they're catching 'em off the docks with angle worms. And the walleyes, those suckers are—"

"I'm here to see you," Gun said.

"No shit." Larry's mouth straightened, and he blinked a few times.

"I need some information about one of your guests."

"Oh?"

"A guy named Rutherford. From Minneapolis, I believe. I'd like his contact information."

Larry went bottoms-up on his beer then set down the mug. He cleared his throat. The grin had dried up. "Sorry, Gun. But hey, that name doesn't ring a bell—and I do make an effort to get to know my clients. Hell, I send them Christmas cards, they're lifelong friends, many of 'em. It's an important part of the business, let me tell you—you want your people to feel like they're part of the family, like part of a team, right? Something you understand, Gun. It's what I try to do here at the Broken—"

"You're forgetting a member of the team, Larry. His name is Rutherford. He was staying here a week ago. Think harder."

"Look, look . . ." The grin came back, a tepid version, and Larry scooted backward on his stool. He said, "Now, even if he *was* staying here—and like I said, I'm pretty damn sure he wasn't—but even if he was, I couldn't pass along that kind of information. My files, you see, they're confidential. Lots of important folks have passed through over the years—people not unlike yourself—and I can't start handing out addresses and such to anyone that asks—not that you're anyone, Gun, but you gotta see my point. I start giving out information like that and pretty soon I lose my reputation and the resort goes to hell. You must understand. You're a guy that knows the value of privacy." His face was running with sweat now, and he drew himself another beer. "Your brew okay, Gun? Hardly've touched it."

"It's fine," Gun said. He was starting to feel badly for Larry. It was no fun having to push a guy who was so eager to please. Gun took a sip of his beer, which was getting warm.

"No hard feelings, right?" said Larry. His grin stopped above his mouth.

"None at all," said Gun.

Larry sighed heavily, then finished his second beer, taking the bottom half of the mug in two swallows.

Gun rose from the stool and walked back to the door, and he stopped there.

"Hey," Larry said. "Leaving already? Your beer . . ."

Gun threw the dead-bolt, and Larry stood up. "Hey, whatcha doing?" he said.

"I'm going to go back into your office with you to help find Rutherford's address and phone number." Gun came around to the back of the bar.

"Gun, really, I can't . . ." Larry coughed and shook his head. He shuffled backward.

"Of course you can."

Larry lifted a hand in conciliation. He wagged his face and the perspiration flew. "I want to help you, but see, um—I told someone I wouldn't say anything about this Rutherford."

"Hedman?"

Larry's eyes said yes.

"Don't worry about Hedman right now. Worry about me."

Larry thought for a few moments, frowning, rubbing his hands together. Then he said, "Shit," and retreated to his office. Soon he was back with a manila folder, which he laid on the bar. Gun took a pen from his pocket and a scrap of paper from his wallet and he copied out the necessary information. When he'd finished, he said, "Thank you, Larry, you've done the right thing."

The man had collapsed on his stool and he was nearly finished with a third beer. He was staring out the nearest window into the middle distance.

"What do you know about Rutherford?" Gun asked him. "What did Hedman tell you?"

Larry shook his head and spoke quietly now, and slowly. "That he was a partner of some kind. Needs to keep a low profile. That's it. Zip. I don't know shit about the guy. Not a piss-poor thing."

Chapter 21

It was four that afternoon when Gun eased the pickup into the shade outside Jack Be Nimble's and tapped a *Let's Go* on the horn. He could still taste the Prince Albert tobacco from the cigarette he'd smoked while talking on the phone with Mazy, who had called as he was about to leave for Minneapolis. Now he'd wait until tomorrow—until after Tig Larson's funeral—to visit Rutherford.

Jack stepped outside, pulled the oak door shut behind him and checked to make sure it was locked. Out from behind his bar, Jack looked even shorter than his five-five and less like a stone Roman than a shaved bear with perfect posture. A poorly shaved bear. His arms were black and his curly chest hair reached halfway up his neck and ended in a crooked razor line.

He climbed in the truck and slammed the door. "You didn't say much, Gun," he said. He held his chin down against his chest. It was his way of frowning.

"She didn't say much either. Just that she had some news for me. Good news. And that I should drive out, she wanted to tell me in person."

"Something about the land?"

"That wouldn't be good news, would it?"

"And you want me along why?"

"Because I don't trust my own judgment. I'm counting on you to see what I can't."

"Don't know if that'll be possible."

"Try."

At the edge of the Hedman land they found the gate wide open, no guards, and Jack said, "They must only do this for relatives."

Lyle himself was standing on the front step in a

relaxed slouch, his thumbs in the belt loops of his creased trousers, his face bright with satisfaction. "Nice of you to come. And you're not alone." Hedman shook Gun's hand, then Jack's. "Jack LaSalle," Hedman said. "Never forget names or faces."

"Lyle Hedman," said Jack. "Neither do I."

Hedman laughed and gave him a slap on the shoulder. Then he whistled, and Rupert came loping up from the lake, the big dog's reddish-brown hair flattened with water. He shook himself at a safe distance before padding over to his master. "Good boy," Hedman said, and Rupert whined, then rolled his yellow eyes up toward Gun and shot lakewater from his nose.

"Where's Mazy?" Gun said.

"She'll be along. I think she and Geoff are upstairs . . . in their room." He shook his head and chuckled. "Hey, let's go 'round back."

They followed him to the rear of the house and into a green safari tent the size of a four-car garage, three walls of canvas and one of netting. Inside was an aluminum table with a sterling ice-bucket that held a long-necked bottle of champagne—*Shit*, Gun thought—and scattered around, a dozen or so director's chairs in all colors.

"Pull up a chair," Lyle instructed.

The men arranged themselves in a generous triangle, and soon a woman arrived with a tray of stemmed glasses. "Thank you, Mona," said Lyle. "I'll pour." But before he'd even started, his plump wife appeared, followed by Geoff and then Mazy.

His daughter looked fine, well put-together, better than Gun had expected, but then she'd never been one to advertise her feelings. She came right up to her dad and gave him a hug, brief and rather stiff—he could feel tension in her back and arms—and when she pulled away, she kept hold of his hand, the strength in her fingers surprising him. "I'm glad you came," she said. "You too, Jack." But her voice lacked its usual huskiness.

Gun wanted to say, 'Enough of this shit. Let's get out of here.' He said nothing.

"We have news for you, Dad, um, Geoff and I do."

What the hell? Gun looked at Jack, whose face was altered suddenly, as if he'd become ill.

"Here," said Lyle, and pushed a glass of champagne into Gun's hand.

Geoff put an arm around Mazy's shoulder and drew her away. For a silent minute the group stood in a loose circle, Mazy staring at the ground between her feet, Geoff grinning at his father, Gun trying to remain upright even as he felt his body tilting like a sailor in a gale.

"Let's hear it," Lyle said finally, lifting a glass. His wife, clutching her husband's arm, imitated his movement, her face a mask of pain.

Geoff brushed a lock of hair from his eyes and blinked a few times. "Really, I think Mazy should be the one to tell —that's what she wants." His eyes angled in her direction.

Seemingly on cue, she lifted her face and met her father's gaze. Without prelude, she said, "I'm pregnant"— nothing in her voice at all, or nothing that sounded like her.

The hell you are, Gun thought.

"Early February, looks like," said Lyle. "Pedersen, you're going to be a grandpa."

Geoff threw back his champagne, Mazy frowned into hers, and Lyle cried, "To a sturdy little boy," and flourished his glass in the air. Hedman's wife took a wee sip, her eyes fluttering.

Later, when Gun had time to think, he would ask himself how he had so alienated his daughter that such a thing might be happening. Was he so inept as a parent that he couldn't see who she was? Worse, had his failings driven her away? And how could she know she was pregnant if they'd been seeing each other for only a couple of weeks—why wouldn't she have said anything? Why so secretive? And what in God's name did she possibly see in Geoff Hedman?

No, it was beyond belief.

He tried to regather himself, concentrate his thoughts, make sense of the babbling around him—first Geoff speaking, and now Lyle, their mouths moving around words that did not register. He tried to find words of his own. He wanted to turn and leave. He wanted to take Lyle Hedman's skinny neck in his fist and squeeze. But more than anything he wanted to wish this moment away, wake himself from it.

" . . . we would have liked this to be different," Geoff was saying. "We were seeing each other in Minneapolis, before . . . it must seem awfully sudden."

Nodding heads.

Roaring silence.

And then Hedman's wife took Mazy by the hand, muttering something about a shopping date, and before Gun was able to speak, Mazy came over, kissed him on the cheek, and was gone—just like that, leaving the men alone in Lyle's safari tent, standing like statues, eyeing each other.

"Please," Lyle said, motioning to the chairs.

Gun and Jack stayed on their feet. Hedman coughed, then whistled for Rupert, who'd been lying in the shade outside, and the big dog loped inside and folded himself at Hedman's feet.

"I'll come right to the point," Lyle said. "You haven't been forgotten in all this, Gun. Mazy insisted that your cabin and the forestland surrounding it be fenced off to guarantee you won't be bothered. You'll have two hundred and fifty feet of lakeshore and plenty of woods. All arranged."

Jack said, "The hell?" and next thing Gun knew they'd left the tent and climbed inside his truck and he was shifting into first and pulling away, listening to his friend, who was thinking out loud, trying to find sense where there was none to be found: "Fine acting job, wasn't it? Hundred percent bullshit, I promise you."

"Maybe," Gun said.

"Not maybe. You'll see."

"Yes, we will. And soon," Gun said.

He turned onto the county road and hit the accelerator and cranked his window all the way down, letting the wind tear through him.

"You're right," Jack yelled. "They've got what they want, and they've got to keep her playing along till after the referendum next Tuesday. But then—"

"If she's playing along," Gun said.

"Damn straight she is. But after that—then what?"

"I don't know," Gun said.

"Exactly," said Jack. "So whatever we do, we've gotta do it before Tuesday."

Chapter 22

"I want to see Jim," Gun said. The woman behind the glass was half hidden by a glossy philodendron vine.

"Dr. Samuelson, you mean."

"Okay." He reached through the window and held the vine aside in order to get a better look at the woman. He didn't know her. She had gray hair piled up on her head like a corn shock. Her eyes were huge behind thick lenses. Her white name tag said EDNA.

"Dr. Samuelson is not here," she said.

"Where is he?"

"He won't be back until . . . let's see"—she reached for a black datebook and riffled through it—"until July fifteenth. He's in Europe."

"And he just left, I suppose."

"As a matter of fact, yesterday."

"Ah," said Gun. "Look, I need a favor."

Edna frowned.

"I want you to check your files," Gun said. "Last week Samuelson examined my daughter, Mazy Pedersen . . . Hedman."

"I know who you are." She touched her fingertips to the top of her gray cone of hair, as if to be sure it hadn't toppled over. She said, "I can't do that."

Gun was still holding the green vine aside. He said, "If it makes any difference, I've known Jim—Dr. Samuelson —for years. He wouldn't mind."

"I'm sorry," Edna said.

"Tell me," Gun said, keeping a check on his voice, "is there any way I could reach him by phone?"

She shook her head. "Not by phone. But there's a forwarding address."

He let the vine drop—but then as he turned to leave he caught sight of an orange dot affixed to the brown purse hanging next to Edna's desk. It was a button that said VOTE NO ON LOON COUNTRY.

"Edna," he said, lifting the vine again, "sometimes it's plain wrong to follow policy." He pointed at the orange button, and she turned and looked at it. "Please," Gun said, "let me see my daughter's file."

The woman touched her fingers to her hair and hummed a low pitch, her lips pressed tight, eyes averted. Then she stood and went to a row of gray cabinets, opened a drawer and riffled through it, plucked a few pages from a file, brought them back.

One glance was enough to see that Samuelson's report verified Mazy's claim, and he handed the papers back to her. "Thank you," he said. "One other question. When did Samuelson make his vacation plans?"

Edna shrugged. "He and his wife go every year about this time. Most people know that."

"Do they use a travel agent?"

"Fredericks, I believe."

An hour later Gun was sitting at his kitchen table, smoking. Fredericks had explained that Samuelson's European itinerary had been on the books for six months —which of course proved precisely nothing. None of it meant anything, damn it. For Lyle, it would have been a simple matter of making an offer as sweet as was necessary, and assuring the doctor that Mazy would later claim to have miscarried. Or at least that's how Gun preferred to imagine it.

He stubbed out his cigarette, took an unopened bottle of Johnnie Walker Black Label from the cupboard, and walked down to the lake. He stepped into the Alumacraft and started the motor. The surface of the water was smooth, and he followed an imaginary line across the width of the lake, past the cluster islands and straight toward the inlet, Woman River, which he navigated for a mile or so, passing beneath the lake road and coming eventually to a second bridge. He beached on a grassy bank, lifted a pair of small battered binoculars from his tackle box, and climbed up the grade.

Ahead, the river widened into a sprawling marsh—hundreds of acres of rushes and cattails, dun-colored mostly, but starting to brighten here and there with shoots of green. The river's main channel wound through the marsh like a string of bright blue yarn. Using the binoculars, he spotted it right away, a couple hundred yards from the main waterway: the dark brown hump rising four or five feet above the tops of the rushes. There were other muskrat houses in the swamp, thousands, but this one was the largest. For some reason, the little creatures chose to build their palace in the same spot every year. Gun had come by every summer to check.

He returned to the boat and motored upriver half a mile, then he cut the engine and with an oar he poled the Alumacraft straight into the heavy marsh. The rushes were thick. It was slow-going, and the sun was nearly gone by the time he got there. Bottle of scotch in hand, he lifted one leg out of the boat and tested the surface of the bog, which felt solid enough to walk on. He swung his other leg over and let his full weight come down. But the crust gave way, and he fell against gunwhale, cracking the bottle against it.

"Aw, damn," he said, amber liquid streaming from a crack that jagged down the glass, neck to base. He raised the bottle and swung it against the aluminum hull, shattering it, then he pulled one foot out of the muck and took a long high step away from the boat. The smell of rotting swamp stung his nostrils. The bog gasped and sucked at his feet.

A few slow steps later, he was sitting atop the firm lodge made of reeds and mud and cattails, watching the day's final light seep into the dark western hills. And next morning, he was still there, watching the sun come around again. It was the second sunrise he'd seen from this spot, and it wasn't as spectacular this time. Ten years ago he'd been less sober, and the glaring colors had looked deeper than blood.

Chapter 23

Stony Lake Community Church was located at the once-picturesque corner of First Avenue and Lake, where the city crew had recently amputated from the boulevards thirteen veteran oaks stricken with wilt. The stumpage invalidated the lush postcards once produced by the Stony Chamber of Commerce, which featured a traditional brick church beneath grand leafy oaks, and the silver-lettered slogan, "We visited Stony Lake. Why don't you?" Now, on a June day bound for an unseasonable ninety degrees, Gun sat on one of the stumps and watched well-dressed men and women file into church. They were here to remember Tig Larson.

"Going in, Gun?" Jack LaSalle was not dressed for a funeral. He was wearing jeans and a dark blue T-shirt.

Gun nodded. "Yup. Don't know if the good shepherd will let such a wolf as you in, what with such a tender flock." He nodded at Jack's attire.

"He shouldn't worry. I'm going in to pay my respects, but I can't stay. Left a sign at the bar that says Back in Fifteen Minutes."

"Be nimble, Jack."

"Ha."

People were already sweating inside. The forty pews —two rows of twenty with an aisle down the center— were nearly full. Men used hankies against their brows. Women fanned themselves with blue-bound hymnals. Reverend Barr was somewhere out of sight. Tig Larson was in a closed walnut box at the altar, the coolest man in the house.

After some twenty minutes the Reverend Barr emerged from a narrow door near the pulpit and ascended into it. All hankies and hymnals quieted as he gripped the stand and glared out over the gathering. He stood stiff for a minute. Then he said, "There's a terrible reason we're here today." Barr let his eyes drop to the podium. "A favored member of this body lies before you," he said. "And his death is one that could have—yes, should have—been prevented."

Gun felt something like a drop in atmospheric pressure as forty pews' worth of bodies inhaled and held it. The barometer's dipping, he thought. Change in the weather.

"All of you know me," said Barr. "You know I'm not a judgmental person. Not one to lay blame on anyone's shoulders. The Lord is slow to anger, quick to forgive, and I try to follow His example."

There were nods around Gun as listeners bowed to the vinelike strength of Barr's voice.

"But this is needless waste, this terrible end our brother Tig Larson brought upon himself. Needless. It makes me angry, and I'm going to tell you why."

Get to it, Gun thought.

"Tig was a brave man," said Barr. "A brave man who stood up and looked reality straight in the face, and in turn decided to face others and tell them what he'd seen."

Concentration was plain in the squints of the mourners. Sweat tracked down their temples, unmopped.

"The week before he died," Barr said, "Tig came to my study with a problem. He said he'd been doing some research. Research into an issue that mattered to Tig in his heart of hearts."

Barometer's dropping, Gun thought.

"There was only one thing more important to our friend Tig Larson than his beloved lakes, trees, and sunshine. And that was the health and wealth of his fellow Stony residents. As a man in a position of leadership, Tig felt it dearly every time one of our locals lost a job or missed a meal," Barr said. He swept the pews clean with a slow staring stroke. "Our brothers in the timber business, feeling hard times. Our resorters, feeling a slowdown in the tourist trade. Tig Larson was a man of compassion, and in the end he decided to compromise one ideal—a natural paradise—to aid another—a prosperous county and community. That was the problem Tig came to me about. He was afraid of the reaction that his public support for the Loon Country development would arouse."

Gun felt a dribble of sweat running like an ant down his neck and reached back to dab it away. Should have dressed like Jack did, he thought, and left just as fast.

"And this is the part," said Barr, "that makes me angry. It seems Tig was right to be afraid. When he came to me, I said, 'Don't worry, old friend, they'll understand. You just go out there and tell them how you feel.' And that's what he did. Not that it was easy for him. But he made a hard and honest choice, and at the public hearing he made his voice heard. And do you know what happened then?"

The barometer fell out of sight. Gun wondered if people were breathing.

"I'll tell you what happened." Barr stood up tall in the pulpit and his sweaty face glowed. "Tig went on home. He went home to take the rest of the day off, and then the phone began to ring. It rang time after time, and every time Tig answered it, and every time it was a local resident, and the residents were mad because of Tig's decision. They called him things. They called him a turncoat. They said he'd betrayed his duty!" Barr slapped the pulpit with both hands.

Lightning and thunder, Gun thought.

"And worst of all," Barr went on, "they never let him explain that they were the very reasons he'd changed his mind." Barr paused, letting the vibrations he'd produced sink into the plaster. "They were hungry, and he offered them food. They were naked, and he offered them clothing. But they rejected all, and that rejection was more than Tig could take." Barr stopped, took out his hanky and wiped the rage from his face.

There it was, Gun thought. The storm, brief but effective. He relaxed in his pew and waited for the rainbow.

It came. "I don't know who among you made those telephone calls," Barr said softly. "But I know this. When you go off to decide for yourselves what we're to do with this poor famished paradise, you'll be thinking of Tig Larson. I want all of you to search yourselves, and if you're part of the problem"—he nodded almost imperceptibly at the walnut box—"then I encourage you to become part of the solution. We can never justify a man's death, but maybe we can make it seem less tragic. We all have one vote to cast. Mine's going for Tig Larson— one last time." Barr was done. He bowed his head to pray.

Gun missed the prayer. His attention was on the reverend's bowed head, which was, as he'd noticed before, bald on top with a ring of gray all around. Before it had meant only that Barr was losing his hair. Now it reminded him of someone else. Friar Tuck. The friar.

People lost no time in getting out of the thick church air. Gun stayed behind until the pews were empty, then walked back past the pulpit and entered Barr's study through the narrow door.

The reverend was leaning back in a fat leather chair, his clerical collar off, his white short-sleeve shirt open at the neck, his eyes hidden under a damp washcloth. Gun's entry had been quiet.

"Very nice talk, Friar Barr," Gun said.

Barr snatched away the cloth and jerked forward in the leather chair. "Polite to knock," he said, with low control.

"So you were at Larson's home, then, right before he died," said Gun.

"What?"

"When all those angry people called him up. Were you there listening, or did he just stop by here on his way to the bluff and tell you about it?"

"I don't know what you're getting at, Pedersen," said Barr. "Tig called me up that day. I was here at the office. He told me what was happening. The next day—well, you know. You found him."

Gun walked over to Barr's desk and leaned his knuckles on Barr's Calendar of Holy Days. "Do you know what I think? I think you could fill a cathedral with the amount of crap you just unloaded out there. I think you know damn well why Larson drove over the edge."

Barr leaned back again, placing the tips of his fingers together in a pastoral repose. "And what about you, Pedersen? What do you know about why he went over the edge?"

"I know he didn't go home to wait on the wrathful citizenry," Gun said. "I know he didn't change his stand on Loon Country because he was worried about resorters. And I've got a very good idea about why he did it, and when I know for sure, a lot of people are going to be disillusioned about the sacred leadership of Stony." Gun removed his knuckles from the desk and stood straight over Barr. "Afternoon, Friar," he said, and walked out of the study.

"Don't call me that," Barr called after him, less control now in the rising voice. "The title's Reverend. Reverend Samuel Barr!" And he sat back in the leather chair, mouth open, staring at the ceiling.

Chapter 24

The next morning Gun rose ahead of the sun, took his swings and swim in the creamy dawn mist, then went inside and made the sort of breakfast he figured could stoke a man through difficult tasks. In a large stainless pan he dropped two chunks of smoked Virginia ham, searing their sides on high heat. When they were sizzling, he cracked eggs onto a cast-iron griddle and cooked them sunny-side up, spooning over fat from the ham. He ate the eggs soft-yoked, with slices of cracked wheat bread. Then he went out on gravel to the lake road. On Highway 71 he turned south and headed for Minneapolis.

Rutherford's street address was 1637 Griswold Avenue. Gun didn't know the area, but he had a map—the one from Larson's Buick, drip-dried, stiff and pocked but serviceable. It placed Rutherford in a residential area near the University of Minnesota. A student maybe, Gun thought. The Reverend Barr, Gun knew, had left a Twin Cities church to come to Stony, though Gun hadn't heard why. Could be that Barr had known Rutherford there and offered his services to Hedman as a tool against Tig Larson. Barr certainly could have been "the Friar" spoken of by the bartender at the Back Forty. Gun squinted his left eye against the rising sun as he drove and tried to think of other men he knew with Friar Tuck halos. There weren't any. But then, he stayed at home a lot.

Ninety minutes south of Stony the lakeside resorts and motels, even the mobile-home parks, began shedding their overpainted, hardscrabble siding for aged wood and cedar trim. Bay windows swelled from clean cabins. The trees grew in ranks, hand-planted, and the grass was clipped right up the bark. This was about as far as most city people were willing to drive on their weekends off, and the city was starting to show. Gun stopped at a small red café with a mug-shaped neon sign and had a cup of coffee.

"You been in here before," said a man with a shiny scalp. He wore a white apron with a jumping bass iron-on.

"Nope," said Gun.

The man eyed him down the counter. "You used to play football," he said.

"Nope," said Gun.

"Well, shoot," said the man, wiping a glass with an apron. "Had you pinned for the guy used to play tackle for the Lions in Detroit. You sure?"

"I live up near Stony," Gun said. "Have had a place there for a long while."

"Well, shoot," said the man.

"Sorry," said Gun. He dropped a dollar next to the empty cup and left.

The temperature had risen enough for Gun to be uncomfortable with only one window down. He leaned over and reeled open the passenger window, then upshifted and drove with the wind crackling in his ears.

So. If Barr really was the Friar, then it made sense to guess that Larson had killed himself to avoid blackmail. Acting as matchmaker, Barr might have introduced the commissioner to Rutherford, then conspired with Lyle to catch the action in a camera lens. A discreet presentation at Hedman's lodge, complete with black-and-white glossies, could have shown Larson the grave error of his conservationist ways.

Gun felt in his shirt pocket and came out with his tobacco pouch and papers. He spread a paper, sprinkled, and rolled a cigarette on his knee. Chances were

Rutherford would have been warned—a call from good old Larry Slacker, probably, or from Reverend Barr right after Gun's post-funeral intrusion. Damn, Gun thought. Rutherford was probably in Miami by now. Walking the beach until the referendum was through, the land overturned, the megamall open, and the condominiums doing a pleasant trade in timesharing blue-suits. And Mazy, permanent daughter-in-law to Lyle. Gun put the cigarette in his mouth and felt in his shirt pocket. He hadn't brought matches.

When the sun was at the top of the sky and turning the highway to water ahead, Gun turned on the radio. A sign told him he was eighty miles from Minneapolis, near enough to pull in WCCO. The Twins were playing the Tigers, game one of a doubleheader. Herb Carneal announced the score, three to one Twins, and the inning, fourth. Gun shook his head.

Rutherford might be gone, then. But there would have to be some evidence of a connection, if there was a connection. If Rutherford was out of town, Gun figured, he'd wait until dark and pry open a window for a look around. He may have forgotten matches, but a four-cell flashlight rode under the seat, next to the Smith & Wesson.

Allan Anderson was pitching for the Twins. With one man out in the Tiger fifth, Anderson walked a batter, then hit another. The hometown crowd buzzed worriedly. Herb Carneal remained placid. Anderson struck out the next two batters. Gun thought about Mazy and needled the speedometer to seventy.

Running through it in his brain for the hundredth time, Gun still couldn't convince himself she was pregnant. In fact, the announcement had only magnified the reason he couldn't believe in the marriage in the first place. She had never shown any interest in Geoff. Not that she hated him—except for that brief stretch after the camping incident. He simply had not mattered to her. He was a thing in the background, an annoyance from the past. And yet she was staying out there with him, wasn't she—for all intents and purposes a new wife and prospective mother? Why, for God's sake? What kinds of threats had been made? And how might they be exposed?

If only, Gun thought, he were sure of his own convictions. Then everything would be easy. He'd simply drive out and get her, proprieties be damned. But he wasn't sure—or not as sure as he needed to be. And for that, there was no one to blame but himself, a father who had failed his daughter in ways too essential to forgive.

Thirty miles from the Twin Cities the Tigers were batting, top of the ninth, one out. Three to two, Twins. Anderson gave up a single, then walked a man, and Kelly went to the mound. Herb Carneal announced a new pitcher, one of the Twins' anonymous relievers, and Gun smiled; he could see it as if he were there in the on-deck circle, working his hands into the handle of the bat, watching the new kid whipping in his warm-up tosses. Smelling pine tar, waiting, feeling the coolness inside. Ready. Herb Carneal gave the batter's name and Gun listened as the first two pitches went wide. On the third, Gun thought swing and the batter swung, sure enough, the ball snapping over the radio and into the space between left field and center. A gapper. Gun turned up the sound, two runs scoring under Herb Carneal's dispassionate voice. Four to three, Tigers, and Gun thought: a happy ending.

He entered Minneapolis in late afternoon and felt the

temperature rise by ten degrees. The old cement towers and the wider, glass-sided new ones trapped the air and held it in the streets. Gun steered the F-150 into a vacant lot and rattled Larson's city map across his knees.

It took him forty minutes to locate Rutherford's house; 1637 Griswold was large and light green and peeling, with the kind of narrow lapstrake siding preferred by the wealthy in the 1930s. It did not look wealthy now.

The house stood next to a four-story brick building with chipboard tacked up over the windows. On its other side were tall, full trees, their lumpy trunks ringed with orange paint. The house itself was in a dark permanent shade.

Gun street-parked directly in front of the house, behind a round-edged silver Thunderbird. If this was Rutherford's car, he was doing all right for a student. Gun doubted that he lived alone. The place was too big. A rental probably, shared with other students. Gun squinted at the dark windows. He was right, Rutherford didn't live alone. Gun could see the movement of several people in the low light, bodies busy with some sort of action. He couldn't tell how many there were, and he didn't want to speculate on what they were doing. But as he watched, a shiny surface flashed for an instant, and Gun immediately recognized it. It was the sheen of a baseball bat, still new with varnish, and it reappeared again and again, swinging downward like an axe.

Chapter 25

The street was quiet as Gun burst from the Ford, vaulted the front end of the Thunderbird, and ran through Rutherford's yard. A few steps from the door he remembered the Smith & Wesson, but he didn't stop. Then he was through the door and twisted screws and hinges were zinging through the darkened room, and two men in light polo shirts stood over a crumpled, bloodied figure.

The one holding the bat was over six feet and thick in the chest and neck. Stunned at the intrusion he stepped backward and opened his mouth, but Gun let his own momentum carry him forward, lowering his head and driving his shoulder into the man's breastbone. It broke his grip on the bat and he hit the wall hard. Gun turned and saw the other man, taller and leaner, moving on his toes like a boxer. He approached feinting with his left fist, then came in hard with a right. Gun caught it and snapped downward. Something gave, and the boxer went shrieking to his knees.

Then came a swoosh of air from behind and a numbing blow. Gun felt an icy slowness spreading through his body. He locked his knees, fighting blackout. In the corner of his eye he saw the man with the bat breathing hard. The man spat red on Rutherford's dark carpet, drew back the bat, and swung.

The action awakened Gun's sunken reflexes. His left hand shot up, palm open to protect his head. It was like catching a cannonball. Bat met flesh with a cherry-bomb pop, icing Gun's forearm. He closed his fingers and found them encircling the bat. It had stopped cold, two inches from his temple. He squeezed the bat and ripped it away, then grabbed the man's shoulders and pushed him into a silver-framed print of *Guernica*, breaking the glass.

"You're working for Hedman," Gun said. "Tell me all of it. Now."

The man looked down at his buddy, who was rocking his wrist and sobbing on the floor. He looked sullenly at the walls. Then his eyes went to the dark door of an adjoining room, and at the same moment Gun heard the soft squeal of floorboards. He dropped his hold and spun, saw two guys dressed in jeans and black T-shirts. One was tall and skinny and carried some kind of a weapon: two smooth sticks joined at the ends by a short chain. The wood was black and shiny. The other guy was short to medium, empty-handed, and had a high-school mustache on his lip.

"You jerk-offs took your time getting in here," said the bat guy, who he'd let go of.

"We been havin' a look. Rutherford didn't keep much stuff around, did he?" The tall skinny one looked at Gun and shook his head. He was holding one of the sticks loosely in his right hand so the other stick dangled free, and now he started a slow wrist motion that made the dangler do unhurried circles. "You're a large sonovabitch," he said.

Gun pointed at the tall man's sticks. "I saw one of those in a movie once."

"Yeah?" A smile.

"Bad movie."

The guy with the ruined wrist had dragged himself over near the door. "How fast can you kill that bastard?" he said, in a voice not soft enough to hide the sniffles.

"Pretty fast," said the guy with the sticks. Gun saw the swinging wood accelerate to a blur, saw a sudden metal

117

gleam in the hand of the short kid, felt his arms yanked back by the guy he'd gone and let go of. His collarbone felt wrong, weak. There were too damn many of them.

"Nice thing about the nunchuks," said the stick-swinger, "you get them going like hell, you can't even see what hits you," but then the front screen door crashed in and Gun could see the nunchuks, could see them perfectly as they came free from the long skinny hand and flew at the ceiling, splitting the plaster. He heard the muffled *whup* that straightened the tall guy up like a post and the second *whup* that brought spray from his neck. There were two more people in the room now, holding silenced pistols. The short kid was dead on his face. The boxer with the broken wrist hadn't even had time to get up off the floor. The guy who'd been holding Gun's arms was out in front now, on his knees.

"No, don't, I got to pray," he was saying to the pistols, but one of them came forward to rest between his eyebrows. Gun turned away. *Whup.*

In the quiet Gun had his first chance to look at his rescuers. If that's what they were. They came toward him, not talking, one wearing a red stocking cap, the other in camouflage fatigues. There was a bitter scent of spent shells and copper.

The man in the stocking cap touched Gun's elbow and pointed to the kitchen. The other man, Gun realized, the one in camo, he'd seen before. It was the eyes. The right eye. The iris was abnormally small, stranded like a little green island on a large white globe. Now the eye winked at Gun.

Gun said, "Hi, Rudy."

Rudy nodded and almost smiled. He led Gun through the kitchen and opened the door for him. A van was backed up to the steps and Gun climbed in and took the chair Rudy offered, a padded office chair bolted to the middle of the floor. Rudy and stocking cap stashed their guns in compartments under the carpeting of the van's floor and sat on benches along the windowless sides.

"Tell me, Gun, how is it everybody remembers my face?"

"A gift and a curse, I suppose." Gun nodded at Rudy's eye.

"How you been?" Rudy said. "Your hair turned white since I seen you last, what, twenty years back."

"After the Series," Gun said. He remembered his confusion that day, answering the door and finding this man standing there, unmatched eyeballs and a comedian's grin. "So tell me. What's Friedrich's stake here? Must be a big one."

"He's Freddy now. Part of the makeover. He'll want to discuss it with you himself."

"So we're on our way to see him."

Rudy nodded.

"Don't tell me we're going to Nevada."

"No, no. Freddy's got a temporary office here. And I think you might like it." Rudy looked toward the front and called to the driver, "Almost there?"

The driver answered with a hard right turn, and then Gun felt the van strain against a steep incline, level off, and slow to a stop.

"Here we are," said Rudy. He reached into his chest pocket and said, "You'll need this." Before Gun was aware of what Rudy had thrust into his hand, the van's double doors flew open and before them, hulking beneath the city's skyline like a bison in a field of dazzling stars, was the hump-backed Metrodome. Gun looked at the ticket in

119

his hand.

"In the mood for a game?" Rudy asked. "Second game of the double-header."

"I never liked warehouse ball," Gun answered.

"Let's go in, anyway."

Chapter 26

The wide cement corridor had T-shirt booths and TV monitors and too many decibels of crowd noise. Rudy stopped at a food stand, bought three brats and handed one to Gun. "That way," he shouted, pointing.

Passing a gate, Gun had his first glimpse of the field. It didn't look like a ballfield so much as an illustrator's rendition of one, the perspective all wrong, everything too green, too distant, too small, the players like little plastic men on a shampooed rug.

Rudy knocked on a gray door in the corridor, and when it opened Gun was looking at Friedrich Cheeseman, who put out his hand. Gun wasn't ready to take it. Not yet.

"A pleasure, again," Cheeseman said. Behind him was a clear Plexiglas wall, and beyond that the field.

"I hope so."

Cheeseman ushered Gun inside and dismissed Rudy with a wave of his manicured hand. His face was lined and leathery and round as an old-fashioned catcher's mitt, but now as he smiled, it turned oval with happiness. He hadn't changed much over the years—a few more pounds—but something was different. Gun couldn't tell what.

"Please, sit down." Cheeseman gave Gun a stuffed chair next to a table loaded with cold cuts, crackers, vegetables, and fruit. "Nice view, don't you think?" he asked, sitting.

Below, Kent Hrbek hit a sharp single to left, scoring Kirby Puckett from third.

"What about these guys!" Cheeseman cried, his manner so easy Gun might have been an old friend with whom Cheeseman watched games every week.

"Good bats," Gun said.

"Damn right. Little help in the right places and they'll contend. I think I might buy them."

"Pitching'll cost you some."

Cheeseman smiled. "I've dealt in arms before." He turned back to the game and swore as Randy Bush struck out to end the inning.

"Friedrich, what's going on?"

"Freddy. Call me Freddy."

"Part of the makeover."

"I've come a long way, Gun." Cheeseman sighed, pouting a little. "I'm respectable. Clean. I don't even throw shadows anymore. Me twenty years ago, me now —two different men. Nobody's got a thing on me. And no embarrassing friends. You see, there was Friedrich, and now there's Freddy. Freddy's on the up and up."

"And the man I met that day in Detroit?"

"That was Friedrich turning."

"All right."

On the mound the Twins' pitcher pumped and fired. The pitch smoked into the dirt at the ankles of the left-handed hitter, who backed away and glared.

"You're right about the pitching," said Freddy.

"I'm ready to hear what you've got to say."

"But you haven't thanked me yet. My driver phoned and said you had your hands full."

Gun waited. Freddy was not a man to be rushed.

The two sat silently through the rest of the inning, then Freddy stood from his padded chair and stepped right up to the Plexiglas, pressed his hands to it and bowed his head for a moment, his shoulders rigid. Then he turned and crossed himself, let his arms drop to his sides. "I had nothing to do with the ugliness, you should know. Let me start from the beginning."

"That would be nice."

"You're familiar with my import business."

Gun remembered the outlet in Detroit. "Banana plants, stuffed cheetahs. I seem to recall a gorilla."

Freddy smiled.

"That's how you met Lyle Hedman."

"Actually, my casino in Reno—he was a regular. We got to talking one time. He asked me all kinds of questions, as if my life was some dark secret I might let him into, and I humored him, naturally. The man's gonna drop a load into the wheel, right? Then it turns out he's into Africa, so I milk him coming and going. That elephant, for instance. I get a healthy cut from the licensing agency, the guide, the taxidermist, the shipping firm—it goes on and on. And Lyle, he's happy as a worm in a shitpile. Anyway, last year he came to me with drawings, market research, all the happy horseshit, not to mention seventy percent financing for what looked like a sunny idea, this Loon Country. So I said sure, I was good for the last quarter, contingent on local support, which he promised was on the way. Just my word, though, no papers, see?"

"What do you know about my daughter?" Gun said.

Freddy put up a hand, his eyes on the field. "Look, Lyle Hedman is a foolish ass. I took a trip north to see his —well, to see your lake, Gun. This was a month ago. He showed me that swampy land he'd purchased, and I told him I didn't like it. Then I saw the politics on the ground— that county commissioner, etcetera. The whole anti-loon campaign. I told Lyle that I never throw money away on shits and giggles. I told him if he didn't find a suitable piece of ground for fantasyland, I'd be upset. I told him to turn the corner with the fucking locals, hire some decent PR. And I had my man let him know I wasn't fooling."

Cheeseman took a long breath then exhaled, fogging the Plexiglas. "Trouble is, Hedman's out of his league. Fucking amateur. No finesse. Setting up the county-commissioner with that poor fella you were checking up on this afternoon? An ugly business. I'm still not sure how he did it—don't know who the runner was. My man picked up the trail at a gay bar, traced Rutherford back here to the city by way of that shithole place on Tornado Lake. When I heard about the suicide, I put a watch on Rutherford's house, thinking Lyle might get nervous, which he did. I don't need any messiness in my life. It's taken me fifteen years to change my profile, and I'm not about to let some dumbass screw things up."

"So where were your boys when my head was getting busted?" Gun asked.

"Lunch break," Freddy said, laughing. Then his face went cold. "And regarding your land—hell, I didn't even know you lived on that lake. Not till my man told me Hedman snatched your girl. That was the last straw. I've stepped away, washed my hands of it all."

"What are you going to do?" Gun said.

Cheeseman turned toward the game again. It was the eighth inning and Berenguer was trying to hold a one-run lead, throwing bullets, enough of them off target to keep the Detroit hitters away from the plate and swinging with cautious respect. "Didn't you hear me?" Cheeseman said, turning back. "I'm pulling out." His eyes were the color and sheen of nickel—hard-gray, and certain. "I sit here asking myself, Pedersen, what would I want if I were in your shoes—if that was my daughter. And the answer? It's easy. I'd want to take care of the matter personally. I'd want the man, and I'd want the man's kid, and I wouldn't want anybody getting in my fucking way."

Chapter 27

He woke up feeling dirt-dried from sleeping in his clothes. He was lying on top of the dark wool quilt, the ripe yellow sun hitting him in the face. He opened his eyes and sought the clock. Six forty-five. He'd had two hours sleep after the drive home from Minneapolis. It would have to be enough.

Sitting up, he felt his collarbone begin to beat like a bass drum where the bat had connected, and he reached for the wall to steady himself. His left hand was stiff as a plaster cast. When the throbbing eased, he stood slowly and stripped to his shorts. The shoulder looked bad, with a black bruise starting at the base of his neck and swelling in a proud arc to where the arm attached. Gun faced the mirror and forced the arm to move. It hurt, but he didn't feel the screaming pain or internal scraping that meant a broken bone. He made the arm rotate, a small circle, then a large one. The hand he paid less attention to. It was his glove hand, still tough from two decades of catching hard-hit and hard-thrown baseballs. Nothing had ever hurt his hand for long. He closed it into a fist, and the pain shot his memory back a few hours.

Rudy had dropped him off, and he'd approached Rutherford's house with caution, his only idea being to reach the truck and head north before anyone decided to pay Rutherford a visit. It was dark, but a bright amber streetlight showed him the house, undisturbed, front door hanging aslant. It seemed strange, a planned murder and four more spontaneous ones, carried out in the middle of a simple, mundane neighborhood. People all around, Gun thought, and not one of them aware of five dead bodies stiffening in a house they'd all walked past a thousand times. He'd gone back inside unwillingly, first putting on a pair of leather gloves from the truck. The room was ripe and the floor sticky under his shoes as he made his way through Rutherford's living room, avoiding the gaze of the scowling dead. Freddy Cheeseman seemed to have Hedman's scheme figured out, or most of it. But he didn't know everything. *Don't know who the runner was,* he'd said. Gun figured the runner was Reverend Barr, the thin Friar—but he wanted to be sure.

After a ten-minute search, he was sure. He found what he sought in a drawer beneath the telephone: a red address book. Samuel Barr was penciled in between The Back Forty and Broken Rock Resort. He slipped the book in his pants pocket and stepped with care to the front door. No one said anything. He propped the screen into a more likely position on his way out.

***

With bacon thawing and coffee ticking on the stove, he broke routine and walked in his underwear down to the lake. No hitting practice this morning—the collarbone deserved a day off. The anesthetizing chill of Stony Lake was welcome. He did a slow sidestroke a hundred yards out, then floated home on his back. On shore again, he noticed a thin pinkness appearing beneath the bruise on his shoulder. His left hand felt stiff but capable. He glanced at the roofless stone boathouse. Later, it would provide therapy.

Breakfast was Wheaties, crushed in the bowl to hasten sogginess, a dull but functional Breakfast of Champions. Gun ate quickly, then dressed in jeans and a red sweatshirt. He looked at the phone, thought of Carol's black bangs and green eyes, and went out to the F-150.

Time for confrontation, Gun thought as he drove to the Hedman estate. Past time, overdue, and calling in the loan. Carol had asked him earlier why he didn't put the questions straight to Hedman's face, the ones about Mazy and Larson and Rutherford. Evidence, he'd answered her then, he needed something tangible. Well, he had it now. Larry Slacker had been shaken loose, and poor Rutherford had paid in full. And there was the new topography of Gun's shoulder, rising up like a tender knoll, big as a slab of sod. That ought to merit a piece of Lyle's busy morning.

When Gun drove up to the iron gate, the jumpsuited guard stepped back a pace from the bars and smiled. He wasn't the same one Gun had throttled earlier.

"Hello, Mr. Pedersen," said the guard. He was taller than the last one, and muscled like a TV wrestler.

"I want to see Hedman," said Gun.

The guard raised his arms in a sorry gesture. "Mr. Hedman isn't here," he said. He was still smiling.

"You might as well open the gate," Gun said. "The easy way or the hard way, I'm going to see him."

The guard hiked the .38 on his hip. "Pedersen," he said, "you used to be a hero of mine."

"I'm glad."

"Used to dread the Tigers' road trips to Minnesota, you swingin' through Twins' pitchers like a wrecking ball. Gave me a thrill, though—I saw you hit three homers off Perry and Kaat in a doubleheader at the Met once."

Gun waited.

"Thing is, though, I don't watch baseball now, and you don't play it. You don't pay my salary either, and Mr. Hedman does. So I wouldn't let you in, even if he was here." The guard shifted his shoulders once, as if he were uncomfortable under the jumpsuit. "But like I said, he's gone. Took the family. Took the dog, even. Caravan of Jaguars, the old man's, the kid's, the wife's. Damn."

Something about the guard made Gun believe he was telling the truth. The part about the Jaguars. He said, "Where did they go?"

"Come on. They don't tell me where they go. They just tell me to watch this gate"—he reached out and slapped an iron bar— "and make sure people on the other side of it stay there." The guard showed Gun a sudden grin. "Another thing," he said. "When Hedman is here, I don't deliver notes."

"Smart guy," said Gun. He got into the Ford, aiming south when he hit the highway.

Driving with his bruised hand out the window, Gun tried mapping his limited options. Time was spinning ahead too fast. He'd delayed confronting the man until he had ammunition, and now that he had it, Hedman was gone. The polls would open at eight A.M. Tuesday, and it was Saturday already and nearly noon. Gun goosed the Ford south on County Road 2. If the Hedmans were anticipating him, the Reverend Barr probably was too. But it wouldn't hurt to look.

Barr lived in an off-white house of European stucco with craggy slopes and ivy crawling a fieldstone chimney. Like Hedman's place, it was invisible from the road. Gun nearly overlooked the black rural mailbox imprinted with domino-sized capitals: S. BARR. The thin gravel drive took him through a tall lilac hedge and into a meadowlike yard. He pulled the Ford up in front of the broad brown front door and left the engine running.

The door had a window and a fat bronze knocker. Gun peered in at a small, wallpapered entry with hanging coats showing from a closet door. A snaggle of wire hangers had been tossed onto a high-backed Shaker chair, and a yellow plastic dog-food dish was upside down on the hardwood strip floor.

Gun gave the knocker three sharp beats and waited. No one home. He gave it three more, and the bronze horseshoe came off in his hand. He walked to the back of the house. There was a long narrow yard, framed at the edges by yellow-blossomed caraganas. Across the yard opposite the house was a cubelike building of matching pale stucco, with square-paned windows. It looked like the servants' quarters in a TV miniseries about nineteenth-century England. Gun squinted through one of the windows. The place was a garage, and it was empty. An oil drip pan sat in the right stall. The floor was swept. Gun could see the swoop and straight lines of a ten-speed bicycle under a sheet of thrown canvas. A strip of twisted gold fly tape hung from the ceiling, bugless.

The sun said it was noon. Gun left the bronze knocker in the reverend's mailbox on the way out.

"They took off," said Gun, "every damn one of them." Jack Be Nimble's was cool and smelled of frying grease. Gun had just finished bringing Jack up to date on the Rutherford killing, the Cheeseman connection, and Lyle's quick exit.

Jack chuckled, rubbing his thick fingers over the black crew cut. "Seems you mentioned that Cheeseman guy one time. Didn't know you ran in those circles, Gun."

Gun looked at the empty bar in front of him. He said, "Aren't those things done yet?"

"Should be." Jack rolled away to the kitchen. When he returned he had two long plates with a shingle-shaped burger on each. Gun's plate held buttermilk in a beer glass.

"Before," Gun said, "I might have been able to just blow in there and get her out. But I waited too long, and now everybody's gone."

They finished eating with no more talk. Gun tucked a five under his plate and got to his feet. "Wherever they went," he said, "I'm going to find out."

"Tomorrow's Sunday," said Jack. "My day off."

Chapter 28

By nine-thirty that evening a rack of washboard clouds had slid over the sky, curtaining the bright new moon and promising a black night. Gun, stiff but strengthened from an afternoon roofing the boat-house, used the last of the light readying the old Alumacraft. He removed any item that might rattle or clank: a pair of loose-jawed pliers under the bench seat, a long teardrop-shaped landing net, a tackle box. He untied the anchor from its rope and tossed it on the grass, then coiled the line and tucked it in the bow, leaving one end secured to the eyebolt in front. He reached into the new boathouse rafters and drew out two long bleached oars, oiled the locks until they swung lightly, and laid them in place. At last he pushed the boat into the water, floated her next to the dock, and rocked her with his feet until the gunwales scooped water. There was no noise but the slap of the waves he'd created.

The straight-line route from Gun's to the Hedman shore was roughly four miles, or about eight minutes in one of the low-slung, high-chaired bass boats that were increasingly populating the lake. In Gun's battered rig, pushed through the dark by a dutiful twenty-five-horse Johnson, it took much longer. At ten-fifteen he was edging past the rocky point that stood out from Hambone Island. Ten minutes later some of the gas lamps that lit the Hedman drive were winking through the shoreline trees. Gun idled down and cut the motor. A chill wet breeze made cat's paws on the water. Gun reached into a pocket of his canvas hunting jacket and brought out a black wool watch cap.

The Woman River exited Stony Lake at the southern

edge of the Hedman property. Moving parallel to lakeshore, Gun rowed silently until he could make out the two ghost banks of rushes that marked the outlet. Then he pointed the boat between them and floated in on the current.

He waited to land until there was a small thinning in the wall of cattails, then dug one oar into soft river bottom and nosed into the weeds. Through scrub-willow branches Gun could see flaring lamps, lit for extra security. The wet breeze blew him the sound of the gas hiss. Gun poled through the rushes until the boat thumped the mossy bank, then replaced the oar and stepped aground. He tied the free end of the anchor rope to a reaching hook of willow root, put his toe to the prow of the Alumacraft and shoved. The boat disappeared like a spirit in the sway of weeds.

The main lodge sat on the crest of a hill, perhaps seventy yards distant and fifty feet in elevation from where Gun crouched in the willows. He was wearing the watch cap over his white hair. He also wore the brown canvas jacket, black woolen pants with dark green flecks, and ankle-high leather boots. He felt ridiculous, but at least he shouldn't attract any eyes.

It took a murky half hour to reach a small, grass-thatched hut some twenty yards from the lodge. He hadn't yet seen a sentry, though he suspected the night guard would be heavy. He sat down in the black shade of the hut and watched for movements in the gaslit yard. Thank God Lyle traveled with his dog, Gun thought. Last thing he needed tonight was Rupert.

He heard footfalls on pavement before he saw the guard. On his stomach in the wide black shadow, Gun's eyes gradually pulled the man into vision. Like the others, this guard wore a light green sleeveless jumpsuit. A three-quarter-sleeve baseball jersey covered his arms against the night. The standard .38 was a proud lump at his side, and a nightstick jumped on a chain at his thigh. The man walked between the lamps on Kenya Drive, headed for the lodge. Gun pulled back behind the hut. He heard the tread of boots on wooden steps, and the chuck of keys as the guard let himself in. When he peered forth again, the guard was returning to the porch. A six-pack of silver cans glowed in his grip.

"Hey, Horseley!" The sudden voice was as high and thin as a nerve in the air. It was also close. Gun tensed his body, strained his eyes.

"Bondy? Where the hell are you?" The first guard, standing on the porch, bent his neck forward, probing.

"Sipping the old man's imported reserves, hey, Horseley?" said Bondy, piercingly near.

"Damnit, where are you?" yelled Horseley. He set the six-pack on a rattan porch chair and used both hands to shadow his eyes as though looking at the sun.

Bondy laughed. "Horseley, you're a blind man. Here. The shed." Gun felt the vibrations of the hut as Bondy slapped the other side of it, not fifteen feet away. Gun rose to his knees and then to the balls of his feet.

"Jeez, Bondy." Horseley sounded relieved. "You blended in. Why don't you get your ass up here and share the wealth?" Absolutely, Gun thought. Get it up there.

Bondy made stiff, musclebound noises getting up. He must have been sitting there some time before Gun ever pulled up behind the hut. Horseley picked up the six-pack and sat in the rattan chair.

"Here's to sudden vacations," said Bondy. He unzipped a beer can and tilted it high.

"Here's to Hedman brew," said Horseley. "The man has taste."

Gun leaned against the dark wall of the hut for the twenty-minute duration of the six-pack. He was in an unfortunate location, since the hut was lit on three sides by the gas lamps. He might go back the way he'd come, but getting anyplace would take too long. He wanted to get into the lodge, not away from it.

"*Grock*," said Horseley, belching mouth open, hippo style.

"All gone," observed Bondy, putting his eye to the top of his can.

"More to come," said Horseley. He stood, quite steadily, and let himself into the lodge.

Chilled from staying motionless in the misty night, Gun set a limit. One more six-pack and he'd take action. Forward or backward, but action. He blew a soft sigh and rubbed his palms. He craned for a look when he heard the porch screen swing to. Horseley was carrying two six-packs.

"Bless you," said Bondy.

The second six-pack was only a fifteen-minute wait. The guards were doing their best not to let it get warm. While Horseley and Bondy giggled the empties into a pyramid on the porch, Gun reached for the layered steel padlock on the door of the hut. Cautiously at first, he rattled the lock against the metal clasp. It made a sound like a squirrel on a tin roof. Bondy and Horseley drowned it out. They were having a belching contest. Gun grabbed the lock as he had Barr's knocker and pounded it against the clasp. He had to do it four times before the sound sunk through the laughter. Horseley put one hand on his gun and the other on Bondy's shoulder.

"Crap, man, did you hear that?"

Bondy grinned a strong imported grin. "Aw, get off it."

"No. Seriously. I thought I heard somebody sneaking around, out by the shed maybe."

Gun knocked again.

"The shed," said Horseley. "Shit. Someone's in the shed, knocking around with the old man's mowers."

Bondy took a step toward the screen door and stumbled over the beer pyramid. The tinkling scramble seemed to tighten their nerves.

"I'm going out there," Horseley said in a beer-amplified whisper.

"Right behind you," said Bondy, whispering too.

Gun flattened his back against the wall of the hut and waited. They said nothing else, but Gun could hear the unsnapping of holsters and feel their uneven steps as they approached. The wet breeze sharpened against Gun's face, and the blue glow of a .38 barrel nosed blindly around the hut's corner.

Gun didn't wait for its owner. He seized the barrel in both hands and jerked Horseley into black shade, the pistol erupting and blowing an orange hole in the air six inches from Gun's left shoulder. The shot startled Horseley into a scream, and for a frozen moment Gun saw the horrified whites of the guard's eyes. He darkened them with a staccato punch to the face and wheeled for Bondy.

Bondy wasn't there. Gun panted quietly for less than a minute before he heard the guard's voice, bleak and sodden.

"Horseley?"

Bondy was close, very close. Gun guessed he was against the adjacent wall, on the corner, too scared to enter the shadow. His finger would be nervous on the .38.

"Come on, Horseley, talk," muttered Bondy. The guard's breath fluttered in his teeth like a moth.

Gun edged to the corner. He thought, I'm a monster in the dark, boy. Then he curled one hand into a searching claw and flung his arm around the corner. It connected immediately with Bondy's soft sweaty neck, and Gun felt the .38 hit the earth. He pulled the guard squeaking into the shade. He was careful, when inducing sleep, not to hit too hard.

Chapter 29

It was cool and still inside the lodge. Yellow gaslight entered through wide windows and landed on the hardwood floor in rectangular sheets. Gun locked the door behind him and stood near a window. The pistol shot had been a bad turn; other guards, posted on Hedman's borders, might be on their way.

After a minute the grounds around the lodge were still quiet, and Gun switched on the four-cell beam and flung it around the room. The gray Hedman elephant straddled the couch and leered into the eye of the light. Gun didn't know exactly what to look for, some sign of Mazy or a destination, but he knew he wouldn't find it here. Not in Lyle's museum.

An arch framed with leather-laced tusks led Gun into a wide hall with doors to the right and left. The right door opened into a factory-sized kitchen large enough to feed a safari, and probably the elephant. The left door showed only a narrower, carpeted hall, with a sculpted walnut door at the end. The door was unlocked. Gun opened it and switched on a light.

A round blue pool took up most of the floor, surrounded by fur-covered pillows of every shape and species. Gun snapped a switch on the wall and the pool roiled up into foam, fogging the air. "Damn," Gun said out loud. On the opposite wall a long peach nightgown hung from the point of a stone-tipped spear.

Upstairs he located Hedman's monstrous master bedroom, an affair made comic by the presence of two separate single beds pushed against opposite walls. More interesting was Lyle's study, which contained a fat oak desk piled with papers and a well-scribbled calendar. Gun studied the calendar by flashlight: no cities, no flight times, no plans. He tried the drawers. One was locked. It gave under an angled kick, and Gun dug down to the bottom through file folders, newspaper clippings, letters. As he closed it, something rattled. On second look he pulled up a plastic-cased videotape. The hand-printed label said, *The Art of Persuasion*. Gun pocketed the tape, shaded the light, and descended the stairs.

Reinforcements had arrived. In the gaslight a stooping cluster of khaki jumpsuits worried over Horseley and Bondy while several fanned out to points near the river. Evidently they reasoned that whoever jumped the guards took immediate leave, instead of staying around. Gun was glad he'd hidden the boat.

He left the lodge by a back door that serviced the kitchen. The sounds outside were panicked: pounding steps searching the bank, face-slapping and grumbling as the two guards came groggily around, quick shouts faintly distorted by breeze. The faint scent of gas whetted Gun's sense of smell, and dimly across the meadowy slope he could see the shape of a squarish, steep-roofed building.

The guest house. If Hedman hadn't held Mazy in the lodge, she might have been billeted there. It was going away from the river, but the gas lamps were fewer here, and so were the guards.

He crossed the meadow staying low and avoiding the patches of weak light cast by the lamps. He heard activity in the lodge behind him, the swearing of sentries. Looking back he saw windows blink on, burn in outrage a few seconds, and go out.

The guest house was locked, but Gun still had Horseley's key ring, and he hit it on the second try. If the guards were sacking the lodge now and came up empty on the riverbank, the guest house would be next. Gun didn't bother to search the first floor. Weren't bedrooms always on the second?

Mazy had been here. The upstairs suite connected two bedrooms with a bath and a kitchen that smelled of spilled champagne. In one of the rooms Gun's flashlight exposed a closetful of clothes, Mazy's size. The bedspread had been yanked in a hurry over humps of blankets. On the stand beside it lay the long red finger of a candle, tipped over in mid-flame, dots of red wax spattered over the wood. Gun searched the drawers of the ebony dresser. They were empty except for a wallet-sized photograph. Gun picked it up. It was a picture of himself.

The other bedroom held less of interest. At least at first glance. Geoff's clothes were squeezed into the closet and dresser drawers, and a long robe hung from a quarter of the four-poster bed. Gun noticed the bedspread, an African print quilted Minnesota-heavy, made into hospital corners. It looked unslept-in. Then he saw what was lying on top of it.

A single sheet of paper, triple-creased, with letterhead and a few sparse lines of type. Against the dark bed the paper glowed in Gun's beam. An itinerary, sent by a conscientious travel agent.

They were in Canada. The agent specified that holders of six tickets were entitled to flights via Northwest to Calgary, Alberta. They'd gone yesterday morning, rising west out of Winnipeg, out of his reach. Gun scanned the paper for a return date and came across another piece of information. Only five of the tickets were round-trip. Someone was staying behind.

A scatter of approaching shouts muffled through the

glass made Gun douse his light. He peered from the window but saw no one. Then the door downstairs slammed open and a rush of boots washed over the floor.

Gun pocketed the itinerary, unlocked Geoff's bedroom window and slid it wide. He grasped a corner of the bed, dragged it six feet to the window's edge, and tied the arms of Geoff's robe around a post. Draped from the window it cut six feet from the fall. Gun lowered himself to robe's length, pushed off the outside wall with his toes, and let go. He rolled ball-to-heel-to-butt on impact, and by the time he reached the river and reeled in his boat, the needles of feeling were beginning to shiver his feet.

Chapter 30

Home. One-thirty A.M. He turned on his thirteen-inch television, jammed the cassette he'd found into the VCR, and stood flat-footed in the middle of the living room floor.

The picture clarified.

Mazy was sitting at a table in a dimly-lighted room, her back straight, arms resting confidently on the carved wooden arms of the chair. On her face Gun recognized the defiance he had struggled against for years. Now she was using it on Lyle Hedman, who sat across the table from her, tapping his long fingers. His lips were moving but there was no sound. Gun quickly stepped forward and turned up the volume, but all he got was a noisy fuzz that masked a low mumble. Mazy shook her head, half smiled, and crossed her arms in front of her. Hedman lifted both his hands in a kind of plea. He leaned forward. He seemed to raise his voice, his face jerking with the movement of his lips, and Mazy turned away. As Lyle continued to speak, he aimed both index fingers at her and the arteries stood out on his neck. Mazy rose from her chair.

Out of the shadows at the back of the room a figure appeared, stepped forward. It was Geoff. Lyle spoke again, and Geoff nodded for Mazy to sit down, which she did. Lyle leaned back in his chair and with his joined fingers made a hammock for his chin. Geoff sat down on his father's side of the table. For several more minutes Lyle continued to speak, his eyes on Mazy, his manner easy and confident. Then he stopped and Mazy gave him a decisive shake of the head.

Now Lyle lifted a single finger and his lips formed the word Watch. He raised his chin and adjusted his gaze to the rear of the room. Mazy turned to see what he was looking at. Two men entered the room. One was handcuffed and blindfolded and being led by the other, who wore the same kind of green jumpsuit as the guard Gun had taken the .38 from.

Hedman said something to the man in green, who nodded and backed his prisoner up against the light blue wall. Mazy turned and shook her head at Lyle. Her lips said no. Her face had gone slack and her eyes were wide, bright with unfocused confusion. Gun dropped into a crouch and pressed the palms of his hands against the floor for balance. He watched the screen and saw Lyle nod his head once and Mazy swing around. The man in green raised his pistol and aimed it at the blindfolded prisoner. From what Gun could tell, the weapon was a .45-caliber revolver. It jumped and jumped again. The man in the blindfold stiffened against the light blue wall, two roses opening on his chest. His head rolled off his neck onto his right shoulder, and the weight of it seemed to settle the matter of which way to fall. He crumpled to the floor. Mazy looked around at Lyle, then at Geoff, who was hiding behind his own hands. She looked back at the man who had fallen, then up at the light fixture above her head, and finally straight into the camera. Intelligence had fled from her face and left nothing to replace it. No fear, no terror, nothing. Gun reached out and touched her, received a small electrical shock from the screen. Lyle stood. His jaunty posture was not congruent with the scene he had witnessed. He and Geoff ushered Mazy from the room.

As soon as they had gone out, the man in the green jumpsuit looked into the camera and stuck out his tongue. He clapped, then reached down and offered a hand to the dead man on the floor, who accepted it and was pulled to his feet, then freed from his cuffs. The two of them commenced a celebration of their performance, mugging for the camera, laughing, and smearing blood on their faces.

Five minutes later, in bed, not feeling tired but aware that he needed sleep, Gun prayed for the courage to make proper use of the destruction rising in his soul.

Chapter 31

The telephone rang early, blistering Gun's sleep. He rolled from bed and answered the phone in his shorts.

"Gun, it's Carol, where have you been?" Carol's voice sounded stretched and wired.

"Carol. I'm glad to hear you." He reached for a kitchen chair and sat.

"I've been trying to get you all week. Damn it, Gun, you worry me."

"I'm fine."

"And lucky. You didn't happen to be playing around Lyle Hedman's place last night, did you?"

"Me?"

"God, I knew it. I knew it was you. The two guards you took out said they got jumped by a gang. Sheriff Bakke believed them, I think."

"How do you know about this?" Gun checked the kitchen clock. "It was only about six hours ago."

"I was up early," Carol said. "I'm a journalist."

"Off the record, then, I'd appreciate your silence on this. Did Bakke tell you anything?"

"Yes. He said apparently there were three or four of you, that you hunted through Hedman's lodge and guest house, that you didn't steal a blessed thing, and that all of you escaped into the rushes."

"That's it?"

"That's it. One thing you aren't, Gun, is klutzy. You didn't drop any clues."

"But Bakke has sworn to 'make the pinch,' right?"

"His words exactly. How did you know?"

"Couple of times a year folks around here get broken into. He always says that."

There was a breath of silence on the line before Gun said, "Carol, I might be needing some help before too long. I don't know that for sure, can't even say what kind of help it might be. Can I call you?"

"You know that, Gun."

"I'd like to think you're in this for more than your dislike of Hedman."

"You know that too."

"I'll call you soon," said Gun. "Hedman's taken Mazy out west. Western Canada. And I don't think he plans to bring her back."

"I'm not sure I follow."

"I could be wrong, but I don't think so. The whole Hedman clan is gone. I think they intend to get rid of Mazy on the trip."

Carol took a sharp breath. "Gun, I know you don't want to hear this, but it's time to get the cops into the picture. If they've taken her out of state, maybe we can get some agency help."

A window patch of reflected sunlight moved across Gun's wall, and his ears picked up the crunch of tires on gravel.

"Where did they take her?" Carol said. "'Western Canada' is a little vague."

"Someone just drove in," said Gun. "I'll call you later."

"Please, Gun. We might not be able to do this ourselves."

"I'll call you. I promise."

An angular blue sedan was sitting in the yard. Gun was startled when the driver slid out and stood, looking uncomfortably around. It was Reverend Barr. He was evidently in no hurry to get to the front door. Gun had time to find his pants.

"Good morning, Gun. I, ah, see you're up." Gun had opened the door just as Barr raised his knuckles to knock.

Barr was clerically dressed in humble brown tweed and a cardboard collar. His shoes were scuffed and apologetic, matching his manner. "Early church starts in another hour or so," he said, his eyes sliding down to his wristwatch. "I thought maybe we could talk."

"Go ahead," said Gun.

Barr's eyes met Gun's for an instant and from there bounced to his chest, forehead, the doorframe, and background behind. They settled at last on a small mole on Gun's cheek, below his right eye. He looked earnestly at the mole. He said, "This doesn't come easily for me. I've a confession to make."

Gun crossed his arms.

"You know what my stand has been on Loon Country," Barr said. "No secret, I've been pushing for it. But things have gotten beyond my control. Beyond anyone's. And I think your daughter's in deep trouble."

Gun felt a willful violence rising up inside. "Talk fast."

Barr's gaze dropped from the mole to Gun's chest, which was nearer his eye level. His voice withered. "It was Lyle Hedman's idea," he said. "Lyle came to me months ago. Flattered me. He said I had the biggest parish in Stony —that's true—and told me I needed a new church. A big one."

"So?"

Barr reddened over the white collar. "Maybe you don't understand. There are better ways of making money than ministering, especially out here in the sticks. But there aren't many better ways of gaining influence. A big church can mean big power, if you work things right."

"So you sold out to Hedman. Should that surprise me?"

"I don't give a damn if you're surprised," Barr said, forgetting his humility.

"Get to the point. Where's Mazy?" He thought, Say Calgary, Reverend, and we've got a match.

"Everything started turning bad when Rutherford got killed," Barr said. "He was our ace. Old friend of mine from the Cities. Used to come to my church down there."

"Mazy," Gun said.

"Please, let me finish. I need to do this."

"Be quick, Reverend."

Barr lowered his eyes to Gun's knees in theatrical penitence. "Rutherford accomplished his purpose. He helped us bring Tig Larson over to our point of view."

Gun nodded.

"Then Lyle got worried. Said we were in trouble if Rutherford ever talked. Said we had to be sure that wouldn't happen. He had it done."

"Why are you talking to me? Why aren't you talking to the cops, if you're so damned sorry?"

Again Barr's weak composure split. "Damn it, Pedersen, I'm telling you because it's your own kid that's going down next."

Gun's arm snapped out in a backhand rope that knuckled Barr across the temple. The minister reeled on his feet while Gun gripped his stiff collar and pulled him up on his toes. "Confession's over," he said. "Now you tell me where Hedman took her, and tell me right, and tell me fast. Or I'll put you on the other side before you've been forgiven."

"Calgary," Barr slurred. "West of there. Then to British Columbia. Hedman told me the whole family was going, sort of a honeymoon trip in honor of Geoff and Mazy. Only Mazy's not coming back."

Gun lifted Barr two inches off the ground. "She's coming back," he said. "Alive. And well." Still holding him by the collar, Gun dragged the minister into the house. Barr sat at the kitchen table with his face in his fingers while Gun fished for an atlas. When he returned and laid it open on the table, a pink, porous knoll had raised on Barr's temple.

It was fairly simple on the map. From Calgary Barr traced a highway across the border into British Columbia, and a winding provincial road into the higher territory of the Canadian Rockies.

"It's the only cabin for a hundred square miles," said Barr. "I pray to God you can find it in time. I wish I had a daughter, Pedersen."

"Lucky for her you don't." Gun picked Barr out of the chair by his collar and skidded him to the door. "Enjoy your last sermon, Reverend. And stay around. I don't want to have to come looking."

"I'll face whatever I have to," Barr said. He managed a sore smile. "I'm ready to make amends. As soon as you get back."

Chapter 32

"He's a damn liar, Gun. How much can you afford to believe him?" Jack was speaking forcefully to break through the noise of the truck, which was barreling northward. When they'd departed Sunday evening, it had been a cool day in June, but the nearer they came to the Canadian border, the more May seemed to step back in. Gun rolled up his window, quieting the cab a little.

"Enough to get me to British Columbia," he said. He looked at Jack, who was sitting straight-backed in the Ford for a better view over the high dash. Jack's chin was tough rock, unconvinced. "I keep seeing that look in Mazy's eyes," Gun added. He had shown the tape to Jack before they left.

"Can't blame you for that."

"Don't worry," Gun said. "I know Barr could've been making it up, trying to get me out of Stony until after the referendum. But I think he was telling the truth. Look at this." Gun pulled the flight itinerary from the pocket of his flannel shirt and shook it open.

It took Jack a moment to decipher the note's significance. He handed it back to Gun, wiped a palm over his black-bristled scalp, and stared forward at the highway. "Five round trips and a one-way," he said. "How'd you get hold of that?"

Gun rolled his shoulders and said nothing, looking straight out over the wheel. He reopened his window an inch and let the wind whistle in. He knew Jack was watching him.

"I heard about half a story on the radio this morning," Jack said. "Early news report. Some gang of vandals on the Hedman place. Didn't steal anything, though."

"Didn't steal much," said Gun.

He had made the drive from Stony to Winnipeg before. Depending on the time of the year, it took between three and four hours to traverse the northwest quarter of Minnesota, then another ninety minutes from the border across the wavy fields and willowy lowlands of lower Manitoba. He'd gone once in late December to pick up Mazy on a Christmas flight from San Diego, and the snow beating across the Canadian prairie had nearly frozen him. He'd put the old Ford into neutral three, four, five times while getting out to heave at the back bumper. But this was June, backing into May, and he was catching a flight, not meeting one. Gun tapped the dash impatiently.

The rattling of the truck and the growing spaces between water towers in Minnesota's extreme northwest made both men thoughtful and anxious. Gun was surprised once to look down and see the needle quivering past eighty. Jack cracked the knuckles of both hands with a noise like the Fourth of July.

"I think she's okay," Gun said. "The round trippers aren't due to come back until Wednesday."

"When this is over, I want Hedman," Jack said.

"I want Mazy first. Then we'll talk about who gets Lyle."

They made the border about eleven at night. A tall, square-shaped guard in a gray uniform stepped out of the concrete customs office. He looked too big to fit back in. Gun rolled down his window.

"Destination," said the guard, shaking his legs one at a time, as if to dispel cramps.

"Winnipeg," said Gun.

"Any alcohol on board?"

"Nope."

"Firearms?"

"Nope."

"Length of stay," said the guard. His feet were planted now, and his palms jammed to his hips. He did a deep back arch, speaking to the sky. "I'm supposed to ask that," he said.

"Forty-eight hours," said Gun. "At the most."

The guard put both hands at the back of his neck and did a round-the-world with his head. "Have a nice night," he said. Gun could hear the stiffness creak in the guard's neck even over the Ford's idle.

"You too," said Gun. He upshifted and nosed the truck toward Winnipeg.

The airport was clean concrete and Sunday-night barren. Gun drove into the parking ramp and took a pink ticket from the humming metal box. "Two nights," said Gun. "Twenty bucks Canadian."

"They have such pretty money," said Jack.

The woman at the airline desk smiled at Gun and told him about the delay. "They're experiencing severe thunderstorm conditions over Alberta right now," she said. "Nobody's flying in at all. There's a snack bar down the hall, to pass the time."

"Nobody's flying in? No charters, nothing?" said Gun. He leaned down close to the woman's orchard cheeks.

"We're in contact with the Calgary airport, sir. No takeoffs, no landings." The woman tilted her face up to Gun's. "And that's it, sir, until further notice. There's a snack bar if you need it."

Gun straightened and sighed and looked at Jack. He said, "Coffee?"

The snack shop had a few round tables and a self-serve spigot that served clear and ineffectual coffee. Jack inhaled at the rim of his Styrofoam cup. "It doesn't have a smell."

A white-faced clock overhead said 9:15. They should have been in the air by now. Gun watched the clouds through the west windows. It would be three hours by plane, another two or three to gather some necessities and search out Hedman's cabin. He shut his eyes, imagining the storm over Calgary.

They drank coffee until a woman's voice came out of the ceiling with the news that flights to Alberta were getting ready to board. Gun's stride made Jack jog to keep pace as they went to the concourse, through the metal-witching doorframe, down the canvas-topped tube to the 727.

The flight began smoothly but got lumpy over western Saskatchewan. Calgary's storm front was carrying east. Jack, in the window seat, appeared to condense, his eyes on the window, a cloudy-milk square.

"First-time flyers," said the captain over the intercom, "think of this as a bumpy road. Lots of potholes."

The 727 hit a deep pothole and Gun felt himself lift briefly from the seat. The belt held him down. He thought, Is this what Amanda felt? The pressure was flat across his hips. He saw Jack's fingers squeeze the armrests. A baby back in coach hiccupped, then howled.

"We're thirty thousand feet above Moose Jaw," said the pilot. "These bad roads should be settling out real soon."

"They buried Jeremy Devitz today," Gun said, trying to see down through the clouds.

"I've been thinking about Bowser."

"Me too."

They landed in Calgary on a blacktop runway slippery with rain. Gun's thick flannel couldn't seal out the chill, and he realized this trip could have been better planned. It was cool down here in the city, and Hedman's retreat was across the border into a province known mainly for trees and altitude. It would be colder there.

"You know the way, right?" said Jack.

"About a hundred miles west," said Gun, "and a mile or so straight up."

The dapper young man at the Avis desk quoted them a low, low price for the Jeep they wanted. "Some places would charge you a third more than that," he said, "and paying that kind of money really Hertz. Heh, heh."

"Thanks," Gun said. He took the keys.

"Idiot," Jack grumbled.

On the west edge of town they located a false-fronted pawn shop with Oriental throwing stars in the windows and a locked rack of guns behind the counter. A woman Gun's age with hair like an orange Lava lamp undid the lock and handed them weapons for inspection.

"What you goin' after?" the woman said. Her voice was Lucille Ball's, a tin scraper. "Moose, out of season. Elk, out of season. Bear, out of season. Hey?"

"Varmints," said Jack. Lucy smiled and turned back to the rack. Her hips hung on her like rucksacks full of birdshot. One of them supported a leather-holstered .357.

"We got plenty of those," she said. "Good luck."

The choice was limited. Gun picked an Ithaca Model 37 twelve-gauge with a Deerslayer barrel, a goose gun modified for slugs. The ammo was heavy and expensive. Jack chose a Savage over-and-under. He bought a box each of twelve-gauge and 30-30 ammunition.

They paid for the guns, leather gloves, and two woolen parkas, black-and-green buffalo plaid. Lucy called to them as they left the shop.

"You two are real cute," she said, waving the bills they'd stacked on the counter. "Now I never want to hear from you again."

As the Jeep left Calgary and began its ascent, the time-and-temp billboard of a stucco-sided bank showed fifty degrees and three-thirty p.m. "Jack," Gun said, "you got a watch."

Jack read his wrist. "Four-thirty."

Gun remembered. "The time change," he said. "We skipped a zone. We've got another hour." Gun leaned back in the Jeep and stepped on the gas. A spray of raindrops snapped suddenly across the windshield, like hand-flung pebbles.

Chapter 33

Samuel Barr had pointed at a highway leading west out of Calgary some seventy miles before swinging north into pine hills. Gun drove the Jeep at hazardous speeds, but the roads were so bad it was almost three hours before they saw the yellow crossroads sign the minister had described. It had been mistreated with a big-game rifle. "One whole corner of it's been shot away," Barr had said, nursing his lump over Gun's atlas. "You gotta take a right."

Gun took a right onto a road deep with sugar sand. Jack flipped open the Jeep's glove box and pulled out a folded road map. He pressed it flat against his knees. "Gee, this is handy," he said. "Florida. Look, a detail of Orlando." He rustled the map back into the glove box. "Gun," he said, "how come Barr knew about that blown-up road sign?"

"Said he'd been out here before. With Hedman. Fishing trip."

"I was thinking," Jack said, "that I really hate being put into the position of having to trust that guy."

"Yup."

"That's the position Rutherford was in."

"Rutherford didn't know the size of the game he'd got into. We do."

The sugar sand subsided as the path led upward, as if the road's entire surface had crumbled loose one rainy night and slipped down the grade to congregate at the bottom. What remained was an adobe-hard trail with craters and black canals that slapped and ground at the four-wheel drive. Gun flipped on the headlights in the thickening dusk. Near the crest of a steep climb a well-tended trail branched right.

The Hedman cabin was nearly a mile through the thick dark pines by foot. The trail would have been easily passable by Jeep, but the engine would announce them like a banner, if it hadn't already. Gun squeezed the Ithaca in his chilled fingers and reminded himself that there were at least five people in that cabin besides Mazy. The surprise would have to be total.

The two of them separated on the walk in, each moving about thirty feet to one side of the trail. The sun was below the rim now. Evergreens shaded to gray. Some distance to his left Gun could catch the occasional glow of Jack's Savage. The pine needles were quiet as corn silk under Gun's boots and sent up the smell of fresh creation.

Another smell gave them their first alert. A slow evening wind reached across Gun's face and brought with it the scent of tobacco. He stopped. Jack was standing stone-silent. Neither moved. The tobacco smell increased with the wind, then faded. They held position and eyed the trees, which grew lighter the higher they looked. Straight overhead Gun could see their tops still getting touched by sun. The smell arrived again on the breeze, and following its direction back with his eyes, Gun saw the source.

A man in a dark spruce Army jacket perched on a stool in a tree stand at the head of the trail. The stand was about nine feet high and constructed of two-by-fours, which had gone gray with weather—a deer stand, Gun thought. Deer were out of season.

It was still light enough to catch Jack's eye. Jack nodded and the stalk began again, slower now. The man in the stand was holding an open-sighted rifle across his knees. His head was helmeted in a cap of rabbit fur. Puffs of smoke floated up from his face and curled off on the wind. As they came nearer, Gun and Jack began to converge on the tree.

They reached the foot of the tree just as the moon peeked up over the hills behind the cabin. The guard looked up at it and shifted his butt on the little stool. Gun reached high and gripped a two-by-four support.

The stand came down with less effort than Gun had expected. The guard gave forth only the noise of an amazed inhale before Jack knelt and put his compact strength into a cheekbone punch.

"He sleeps," Jack said, standing. He shook his hand, fingers splayed. "Ow. All that sneaking around kind of wound up my spring."

They emptied the guard's 30-06 and tossed the shells into the trees. The cabin was a Hedman-sized structure of stripped logs standing off across a wild-flower clearing. A yard-light burned next to a square woodpile. Someone had started a fire, and the smell of smoke and coffee lifted from the chimney.

"We'd better stay back," Gun said. "Far enough in so we can't be seen from the yard. We'll take the cabin from the rear."

"They might have another guard up somewhere."

"Maybe. I don't think they'd stick two guys up in trees."

The low-profile hike kept the cabin in constant view and took another thirty minutes. The moon was an indistinct platter behind the haze when they reached a set of red pines twenty yards off the back porch.

"Let's go in like wild men," Jack said softly. His cheeks were ruddy as a child's, and Gun thought he could feel a schoolground heat come off him. "Butch and Sundance," Jack whispered. He was crouching, as wide in that position as he was tall.

"You go around to the front door," said Gun. "I'll get up on the back porch. We'll meet in the middle."

"See you in five," Jack said, and he went, the Savage riding comfortably in his hand. He reached the left rear corner of the cabin, paused there, threw a grin back at the trees. It made Gun wonder at their bravado. Three, four rifles at least inside that cabin, and he and Jack outside, talking like third graders about cutting down enemy cornstalks. Butch and Sundance.

Now Jack was gone from sight, rolling up the left side of the cabin, moving fast to reach the door. Gun stooped only slightly—if anyone were looking, six-and-a-half feet would be seen whether he was bent over or not—and made the porch. Like everything else Hedman owned, the cabin was well-built. The porch boards didn't creak under Gun's weight. He crept to a window, tilted a glance inside, saw three men at a knotty-pine table. They wore buttoned underwear shirts and black suspenders. Real lumberjacks. They were eating ham steaks. Gun wondered where Lyle was, wondered if Lyle was even along, and then he heard the door.

It slammed at the front of the cabin, and at first Gun thought Jack had gone in. But there was no noise afterward. Gun moved across the window and stood next to the porch door, his back against log siding. If anyone had come out, he hadn't seen Jack. There was no disturbance. Gun gripped the door handle and set himself. He pulled the Ithaca ready. He was taken by surprise when someone tall, not Jack, appeared in his corner vision.

"Hey!" the guard yelled. He was evidently surprised too, but recovered quickly enough to unholster the .44 at his hip.

"Drop it," Gun said. The Ithaca was aimed. The tall man did not register the action. He fired the pistol, and Gun felt hot teeth tear at the flesh of his left ribs. He stayed steady and shot the guard through the chest.

At once the air was soaked with noise. Dark roars as the lumberjacks seized their guns, the steely snap of a rifle from the front of the cabin, yells crowding each other for help. Gun's ears pulled Mazy's voice from the mob. He pumped a new slug into the chamber and put his shoulder to the door.

The lock broke on the second blow and Gun swung in off balance. A white-faced guard, braced before a door on the right-hand wall, took hurried aim and fired. The Ithaca snaked in Gun's hand and came up with the stock blown off. Gun flung the barrel at the guard and dove for the nearest cover, a wide woodstove that stood out from the wall. The guard's shotgun blasted again but the stove sent buckshot rocketing. The stove was hot, and Gun was grateful for his thick woolen coat and gloves. Through the hell of shotgun roar Gun could feel the shake of cabin walls, as though a bear were belting the logs. He heard a wild barking laugh outside. He heard, from somewhere behind the panicked guard, a willful angry scream from Mazy. The scream tore at a nerve of memory and pain, and Gun stood without thinking and gripped the stove in his leathered hands.

The guard howled as Gun raised the stove from the floor. Rivets made peeling metal shrieks as the chimney flue came in two. An elbowed section of twelve-inch pipe hung on the wall, dropping cinders. Gun staggered forward, the stove out front. The guard fired once more before Gun reached him, and this time several pellets struck his legs. The stove became impossibly heavy. His hands and chest smoked against the black iron. He felt himself come near the guard, heard the man's howl, and then the stove came down. The guard was silent beneath the woodstove, which sat angled on its side and coughed up ashes through its broken spout.

"Who's out there?" quailed a voice. It came from behind the door where the guard had stood. Gun recognized it.

"Just me, Geoff," he said. "Now get my girl out here before this place burns." Live sparks were spattering from the stove. One flamed up in the sleeve of the guard. Gun stamped it out.

"Dad?" The lock clacked, the door inched open. Gun heard Mazy's voice, but Geoff's face filled the crack.

"She's okay, Mr. Pedersen," said Geoff.

Gun didn't answer. He pushed through Geoff and saw Mazy sitting on an ill-made bed.

"Dad. You're hurt."

They heard the front door slam and Jack coughing as he went past the smoldering stove. "Mazy! You're okay?" He caught sight of Geoff, on his butt in shock, and looked at him as though considering a kick to the crotch.

Geoff spoke slowly from the floor, head in his hands. "You guys are nuts."

"Shut up, Geoff," said Gun, looking at Mazy. "You aren't here at all."

Chapter 34

"Did they hurt you?" Gun said, on his back. Mazy was dabbing at his ragged side with a cloth, which made him pinch his words.

"I'm all right. Believe me." She kept her eyes on the wound. "This is ugly. What did he shoot you with, a cannon?"

"A .44, and I'm glad he was in a hurry," said Gun. Jack had doused the gutted stove and opened windows to clear the smoke. Gun was on the bed.

"I didn't have any choice, Dad. I hated all the lying. They had me, was all." Mazy gripped Gun's wrist for a moment, suspending the rag above the ripped skin. "But you knew that. You could tell." Gun reached up and ran a finger along Mazy's cheekbone. She stopped it with her hand. "Couldn't you?" she asked.

"You could've been less convincing."

Mazy wiped hair from her forehead with the back of her hand. "It must have been rough on Barr's ego, coming to you and spilling it like that. All part of the production, just to get you out here."

"What about the rest of it? You and Geoff."

Mazy shrugged, a slim-shouldered gesture like her mother's. "Marriage papers are real enough. But there's no marriage. No baby, either." Her face went from relief to anger. "Won't Lyle's family doctor be surprised."

"Will be, when he gets back from the Riviera. Where's Hedman?"

"Might be anywhere. He drove out of Stony behind Geoff and me. Annison drove separately. Always does."

"Annison?"

"Lyle's wife," Mazy said, pausing for a glance at Geoff,

whose face was dark. "Geoff's mother."

Gun glared at Geoff, who was sitting up straight now, his arrogance returning. Mazy rinsed the cloth in a basin. When Gun's side and legs were clean and wrapped, the four of them walked away from the cabin toward the road.

The Jeep pulled into the Calgary airport at eleven p.m., midnight in Stony. Gun booked four one-ways on American to Winnipeg. Then he went to a pay phone on the wall next to the flight desk. He reached Carol at the newspaper office on the ninth ring.

"Where in hell are you calling from!" she blew. "No. Don't tell me. I think I know."

"What did you expect?" Gun said.

"Damn it, Gun, you like doing this!"

"Mazy's all right. So is Jack."

Carol said, "This isn't how it's supposed to work, Gun."

"I'm all right, too. Thanks for asking." He told her about Barr's confession, about the sudden flight, about the cabin in the woods with Mazy inside it.

"If Barr told you all that just to set you up, then how did you get out of there? And with Mazy?"

Gun shut his eyes, inhaled.

"Did you get hurt? Did anybody get hurt?"

"Carol, three of them are dead. None of them were Hedman."

"My God."

"I need your help now. All of us do."

"What can I do?"

"Is it possible to put out a special edition of the *Journal*? Can you fire up the presses a little early?"

"I can if I need to. I'll have to do it without my regular help."

"It's important, Carol." Gun gripped the phone too hard, and his palm, red as fire, opened without permission. He caught the receiver with a forearm against his chest and juggled it back to his ear. "We have two witnesses now, Geoff Hedman and Barr. First you've got to secure Barr. Get him out of commission."

"Out of commission."

"Lure him in, knock him out, lock him up. Somewhere. Keep him cold until we get back. We're going to need him."

"I'll try." Carol sounded winded. "What about the paper?"

"I want you to write an article. News, editorial, call it what you like. People read your paper. Tell them how their good reverend got his buddy Rutherford to set up Tig Larson, and then let him go down under Hedman."

"Hold it, Gun." Carol was scribbling audibly. "If I do this, if I print this, all of it had better come out. In court. If one fragment of this isn't proven, I'm throwing twenty years of news work out the window."

"It'll stick," Gun said. "If you're afraid, don't write the article and we'll get through it another way. But Lord, Carol, it might make the difference."

"Difference in what? You've got a witness with you. Bring him home."

"The difference might be whether Hedman goes to jail, or I do. And Jack. We just left a few of Hedman's pals out in the woods, but he has a lot more. In strategic positions, I'd bet."

Silence from Carol.

"If you write it," he said, "include everything. Don't leave anything out. Only the unabridged version will do."

Carol's voice was dark and sharp, obsidian. "When will

you get back?"

"Tomorrow afternoon. We're flying to Winnipeg on American. We'll drive from there."

"Drive fast," Carol said.

Chapter 35

The DC-10 touched down in Winnipeg at one-thirty. The sun was starting to burn a hole through heavy skies, a silver drizzle was angling down before a clearing west wind, and Carol Long was waiting at the airport. She was the first person Gun saw as he and Mazy stepped from the jetway. He was surprised at the rush of joy he felt at seeing her. She wore a bright red sweatshirt. Her hair looked coal black. Her face was drawn and pale. She swept past Gun and threw her arms around Mazy. Then she pulled away and touched Mazy's chin with the fingertips of both hands.

"And you came through it fine," Carol said. "Thank God." Her eyes were dry and steady, but there was a slight tremor in her chin.

Jack came down out of the tunnel flattening back his greasy crew cut with both hands. He smiled at Gun, then at the women. Geoff stood looking at his feet.

Gun said to Carol's back, "How'd it go last night?"

"Fine," she snapped, turning. "I did everything exactly as requested." Her glare was brief and freezing.

They stopped at a gun shop, then headed south for Minnesota. Gun and Mazy rode in Carol's car, Jack followed with Geoff in Gun's pickup. By three-thirty they'd been on the road half an hour and Mazy was curled sleeping in the backseat. Gun was driving, holding the wheel lightly because of the burns on his hands. He sipped at a cup of coffee he'd picked up at the airport.

Carol was silent and staring out the passenger window at the long, greenish-brown reach of Manitoba prairie. So far Gun had honored her apparent wish to be left alone, but now he cleared his throat.

"So you don't feel like talking," he said.

She ignored him.

"Because I left without telling you what was up."

"Your daughter's trying to sleep," Carol said.

Gun looked sideways at her, rubbing the unburned heel of his right hand against his two-day stubble. He said, "Do you think I would have done what I did if I thought there was a better way?"

Carol looked at him, and their eyes met for an instant before she turned away. "Probably not. But I don't think that says much for your judgment." She brought up her feet and curled into the seat, facing the passenger door.

"Fair enough," Gun said.

The drizzle had stopped, but the sun was nothing more than a dull yellow beach ball in the gray sky. Gun could tell by the arch in Carol's shoulders that she wasn't anywhere near sleep, and her left hand, resting on her leg, was a hard white fist. "Carol, maybe you ought to tell me what happened last night. This isn't over yet."

"I'd better," she muttered into the window. She twisted around in her seat, pulled herself upright. "I wrote the article, took it to the printer, and locked up Barr in a safe place." She spoke quickly, then clamped her mouth shut.

Gun blinked. "You actually locked him up," he said. He saw Carol start to smile.

"He's in your new boathouse," she said.

"Lucky I got the new roof on it." He smiled and swung into the passing lane to overtake a truck pulling a hay rack loaded with scrap iron. He laughed, trying to picture it: Barr in his stiff black-and-white collar and his carefully pressed pants, sitting there in the dark on the dirt floor, or maybe in the old Alumacraft, on one of the life cushions. Getting some good practice in sincere prayer. "How'd you get him in there?"

"I had good help." Now Carol smiled in spite of herself. "My son showed up last night, at supper-time."

"No kidding. From California."

"He wanted to see the 'rugged north country.'"

"Turned out more rugged than he expected."

"I'd say so." Carol's voice had lost its tightness, sounded natural again. "Mike and I drove over to Barr's house. No one was home, so we tried the church. There was a light in his office. I left Mike in the car, and he covered up with a few blankets and coats in the backseat while I went to Barr's door and knocked. When he saw me, he lit up like Christmas. You know his capacity to gloat—here it was, the night before the referendum, victory just hours away, the new cathedral probably cementing itself together in his fantasies—he was thrilled to see me. Asked me in for coffee. I told him thanks, but we had something to discuss. Someone had leveled serious charges against him, and I wanted to hear his side of the story before I wrote it up." Carol paused, gave Gun a self-satisfied smile. "I was winging it. Had no idea what I was going to tell him. I just wanted to get him out to the car. Finally I said that one of Hedman's people, the cook, had phoned me up with a story about bribes and collusion. The reverend sobered up in a hurry. I said I'd arranged to meet the cook at my place, and would he like to come along. So off we went."

Gun swallowed the last of his cold coffee and grinned into the cup.

"Then we took Barr out to your boathouse. I think Mike's still in shock. His mom, the conspirator."

"How'd you get it open? I had it padlocked, I think."

"Before Mike and I went over to Barr's, we stopped at

old man Calvert's, borrowed his lock clipper and bought a new one."

"So Barr's waiting for us."

"He's waiting, all right. The question is how we're going to reach him." Carol sighed, then looked at Gun hard, her pupils bright as knife points. "This is the part I haven't told you. Hedman's got roadblocks on every road leading into the county. My paper hit the stands at eight-thirty this morning, and you'd better believe it caused a stir. Hedman called me at a quarter to nine, just before I left. Threatened to have me arrested."

"For what?"

"He wasn't too specific."

"Tell me about the roadblocks."

"Like I said, every road leading into the county. Highways, township roads, everything. Tar and gravel. The official version is 'suspected felons' in the area; Sheriff Bakke loves his sweet ambiguities. But Hedman's had every one of his paper-mill workers deputized. He's taking no chances."

"I'm flattered," Gun said.

They drove on under overcast skies, crossed through customs without incident and continued southeast, the low marshland of the northern counties stretching out on both sides of the road, the real pine country still a hundred miles off. Half an hour beyond the border, Gun pointed at a green sign that said, HOPE, 5 MILES. "There's a good little café there," he said. "Anybody hungry?"

"I am," said Mazy from the backseat. She sat up and leaned forward, pushing her face between the bucket seats. "You two look nice together," she said.

Chapter 36

Gun parked in front of a small brick café on a mostly boarded-up Main Street. The sign painted in red letters across the big picture window said FAT FREDDIE'S. In smaller letters below, it said *Post Office in Rear: Hope, Minnesota 56362*.

"You sure about this?" Carol asked.

"Freddie eats his own cooking," Gun answered.

They got out of the Horizon and stretched. Jack and Geoff came rumbling up in Gun's pickup. Gun walked to Jack's window.

"Geoff behaving himself?"

Geoff leaned forward. His face had gotten older on the drive. "You guys are done," he said. "All done. You might as well let me off here."

"Surly child," said Jack.

They were given the window booth. The place wasn't particularly clean, but the burgers were thick, the buns homemade. Fat Freddie was nowhere to be seen. Gun ate quickly and finished first, then gave a summary of Carol's news from Stony. As he spoke he took out a small pearl-handled jackknife and started working on his fingernails. "Hedman might have all the roads into the county sealed off," he said. "But there's another way in. The northern tip of Stony Lake juts over the county line. We need to reach the lake, find a boat, and head for my place. We pick up Barr and motor on into town, right up to the docks at the Muskie Lounge. If the referendum's passed, and you can bet it will have, the celebration will be in full swing."

"Where's the boat going to come from?" Carol asked.

"There are lots of good boats up there on the north end. We'll get a friend to lend us one."

"It might not be so easy for you to find a friend tonight," Carol said.

"Maybe not," Gun agreed. "But when I need to, I can turn on the charm." He pointed his jackknife at her.

"You'll need to."

"You watch," Gun said.

The waitress came with the check and set it down in front of Jack, who slid it over to Gun. "Your treat, right?"

The waitress at the till now was older, with red eyes and orange lipstick. "Your face," she said, waving the twenty Gun handed her. "I could swear I've seen it."

They left. Gun was following Geoff down the sidewalk when suddenly Geoff turned. He said, "I really need some cigarettes. Mind if I run back in?"

"Didn't know you smoked."

"Only when I'm nervous."

"I'll go in with you." Gun steered Geoff back inside by an elbow.

Geoff asked the woman for three packs of Camels, then picked up a pen from the counter and started writing a check. Gun stopped him and paid for the cigarettes with a five.

"Let's go." He took Geoff's elbow, but Geoff pulled away.

"I should use the can," he said, his face verifying the urgency in his voice.

Gun waited outside the men's room. "Feel better?" he said when Geoff emerged. Geoff only shrugged.

Back on the road, the barren lowlands gave way to an occasional hill populated with scrub pines. The wind seemed to be coming from the west and south at the same time, and Gun suspected about sundown it would switch around to the east. The thinning cloud cover would firm up and drop down low, making good darkness.

Mazy was in the front seat now, Carol in back. It was the first time Gun and Mazy had been alone together since the rescue, and they talked quietly while Carol slept, telling old family stories. The memories were fresh tonight, pleasant to dwell on, not painful, Gun realized.

"I'm sorry I missed so much," he said.

"It's okay." She leaned back on the headrest and smiled at the ceiling. "Mom said something once, late in the summer. You were on a road trip."

"As usual."

"She told me that missing someone you love is a privilege."

"She was right," Gun said.

Silence. He looked at his daughter, who smiled thinly, turned away. She said, "Sometimes I wasn't sure if you missed her at all. I was afraid the only thing hurting you was the guilt. I wanted to think it was love too."

"Both," said Gun. "A lot of both." He swallowed hard, trying to relax the swelling in his throat, afraid to let himself speak again.

Chapter 37

Gun slowed the car as they neared the crest of a long climb, dark trees rising on both sides, headlights spearing the low gray clouds like a pair of giant white fingers. Then the road flattened out and Gun pulled onto the gravel shoulder. On a clear night the view from here would be magnificent, an endless reach of black forest, dotted here and there with lights and cleft in two by the liquid expanse of Stony Lake. But the wind had shifted to the east, as Gun had expected, and tonight not a light was visible. He shut off the engine and rolled down his window. As if wakened by the silence, Mazy sat up from sleep. No one spoke. Gun could smell the lake. He could feel the cool late-inning buoyancy in the space beneath his heart.

The rumble of the pickup approached from behind. Headlights illuminated the inside of the Horizon, and Gun got out and walked the ten yards back along the gravel shoulder to talk with Jack.

"Let's park in Landsom's gravel pit," Gun said. "We can walk from there, through the federal land."

"You got any ideas about a boat?"

"Yup."

"Let's go, then."

Gun led the way. He continued half a mile on the county road, then took a right and went a quarter mile on township gravel. Just past an empty farmhouse he turned right again, then followed a curving, rutted drive that cut through heavy woods. The gravel pit was about a hundred yards in, an old dig no longer used and overgrown with weeds. It looked like a moon crater. At the far end was Landsom's rusty combine, sitting there as it had for years.

"We'll walk in from here," Gun said. He parked behind the combine. "It's only a quarter mile to the lake. Straight that way." He pointed into the woods, due south.

Jack pulled up alongside in the pickup. Gun walked back to the trunk of the Horizon, opened it, brought up artillery. The Savage over-and-under, a Remington 870 twelve-gauge he'd picked up in Winnipeg, boxes of shells.

"You said this was going to be easy," Carol said, slamming the door and striding toward Gun. "Get a boat, pick up Barr, cruise into town. Nothing to it."

"That's right."

"So what are those for?" She pointed at the guns.

Gun didn't answer. Jack leaned into the bed of the pickup and held up a long fish-cleaning knife in a leather sheath. "For you, Carol. Just in case." He reached over and slid the blond-handled knife into the front pocket of her jeans.

Carol stroked the knife's handle and frowned. "What kind of trouble are you guys expecting?" she asked, a ripple in her voice.

"Maybe none," Gun said.

"Maybe more of what we had out west," Jack added.

Carol's eyes were on the shotguns and troubled. She said, "I'm afraid having weapons along will only make things worse. Gun"—she drew the fish-cleaning knife from the sheath in her pocket, its blade long and slightly curved—"I'm starting to think you really want this. A physical confrontation. You and Lyle . . . and the law of the jungle." She shot Gun a sarcastic smile.

Gun handed the Savage across to Jack.

Carol said, "Mazy, can't you see what's going on here?"

Mazy shook her head. "I don't think you know what kind of people we're dealing with."

"The kind of people we're dealing with? We're dealing with a bunch of hired deputies, and none of them are the least bit interested in doing us any harm." Carol ignored a chuckle from Jack.

"That's right," said Geoff. Everyone looked at him. He kept his face on the level and his shoulders high, but took a step backward.

Jack said, "Geoff's the only person agreeing with you, Carol."

"You've all got an inflated idea of Lyle Hedman's power," Carol said. Her eyes were bright and her face shone with anger. No one answered.

Gun slid the pump action of his Remington back and forth twice to be sure it wasn't jammed, then thumbed four shells into the magazine, pumped one into the chamber, filled out the magazine with number five, and checked the safe. He looked around the circle of faces. "Time to see about that boat," he said.

Jack loaded his shotgun and they started off, Gun out front, Geoff sandwiched in mid-file, Jack in the rear. The forest was old and relatively free of undergrowth, and in ten minutes they could see Old Stony Road. The lake was twenty yards beyond it, hidden now by fog rising off the water.

"You all know Lou Young's place, right? It's his boat I'm thinking of. Old Glastron, built like a tank, big Merc on the back. He keeps it on the lift. If I know Lou, it'll be unlocked." Gun glanced around at each face. Jack's chin and cheekbones looked hard as cement. His eyes twinkled like spots of polished granite. Geoff seemed thoughtful, almost confident, gazing off in the direction of the lake. Carol's eyes were dark slants. Half her mouth was turned up in a skeptic's grin. Mazy's face was placid and beautiful, but Gun knew if he touched her arm he'd be surprised at its hardness. As a small girl she'd smiled dreamily through all her inoculations, yet more than one doctor had broken off needles in her tough little muscles.

"Okay," Gun said. "Let's stay well back from the road until we're opposite the grove of maples at the east of Lou's property. Then we cross over the road and walk the center of the grove to the lake. From there it's only forty yards to the boat. The bank is steep. We stay low and Lou needn't see us."

"I thought your charm was getting us the boat," Carol said.

"As it turns out, no." He motioned with his head and started walking. Across the road from the maple grove they gathered in the darkness below the spreading limbs of an oak. Two sets of headlights passed by. One was a county sheriff's car, headed toward Stony.

"Out of his jurisdiction," Jack said.

Dark again, they crossed the road, stayed to the middle of the grove and made the lake. The water was sheltered from the wind here, and the surface shone with a dark luster. To the right, barely visible in the fog, was a small boathouse. Young's heavy runabout hung in front of it, suspended just above the water on the square metal lift.

In a low crouch Gun started toward the boathouse, Carol and the others following. At its near corner Gun was stopped by a soft, low growl. He reached back and put a steadying hand on Carol's arm, strained ahead to see some form or concentration of darkness. There was nothing. A dog? Lou had never owned one, Gun was sure of it. Scavenging coon, maybe. Or mink. He'd heard a growl like that once, a thirty-five-incher, its foot in a trap. He took a slow step forward and his boot snapped a twig. Then a throaty roar exploded in the air, and a shadow of liquid motion leapt from the opposite corner of the boathouse, eyes glowing yellow, body cutting the night like wind. Gun braced himself and brought up his shotgun like a staff. The yellow eyes flew at Gun's neck. Something snapped. There was a hard thump, a choking sound. A floodlight kicked in, washing the lakefront white. A German shepherd lay at Gun's feet, coughing, back legs splayed, front legs pawing at the chain around its neck.

"The hell's going on here!"

Lou Young's lanky figure stood on the sloping ground between his cabin and the boathouse. Gun started up the hill toward him, alone.

"That you, Gun?"

"Sure is, Lou." Gun walked up to him. White curls stuck out from under Lou Young's camouflage hunting cap. He was sucking on a short fat cigar. His old face was nothing but bone and shadow.

"Didn't know you had a dog, Lou," Gun said. He set the stock of his Remington on the grass.

"Don't have a dog," Lou said. "My sister's. She's off for Arizona these two weeks." Lou tilted his head and shot a stream of smoke straight up. "Got a nasty voice, though, don't he?"

Gun nodded. "You're not in town for the doings, Lou."

"Nope." He squinted at Gun. "But I guess you're on your way."

"Yup."

"And you want my boat."

"That's right."

"Hedman's got some money on your head, Gun. Not exactly official, but folks know. Five grand to the man who gets you on a leash." Lou took the cigar from his lips, hawked, and spat.

"What do you think about that, Lou?"

"I think the man who'd take it's as bad as the one offerin'." Lou looked from Gun to the lakeshore and nodded toward the boat. "Fresh tank of gas. Choke her down halfway till she's warm."

"Appreciate it," Gun said. He turned to leave.

"There's lots of folk like me around," Lou said. "Don't say a hell of a lot. Tend to stay out of things, like you. But they can't jerk our heads too easy, neither."

Without turning, Gun lifted a hand in reply and walked back down to the shore. "Lou says we can have the boat," he said.

"Charming," said Carol.

They boarded and motored off into foggy darkness, the German shepherd setting up a high, mournful howl that pierced the heavy drone of the big outboard. It was a ten-mile trip by water to Gun's place, half an hour. Jack drove. Gun sat close to the starboard gunwale and let his burned hands slice through the cool water. Off Crow Point half a dozen boats worked the walleye hole, but they were mostly alone on the lake, or seemed to be. Poor visibility. No moon, no stars. Just the ragged fog that hung in wispy shreds above the water. The wind had stalled out and the ride was smooth.

They reached Gun's dock at ten-thirty, according to Jack's illuminated watch. Mazy tied up the boat.

"Got the jail keys?" Gun asked Carol.

She held up a ring.

They walked to the boathouse and gathered in a semicircle at the door. Jack said, "You hungry in there, Reverend?" Carol put the key in the padlock. It didn't snap

177

open. She tried again, shook it. Nothing happened.

"You sure it's the right one?" Gun asked.

"Positive."

"Here. Let me try." Gun leaned the Remington against the wall next to the door, inserted the key and yanked. The lock held. "You all right in there, Barr?" he yelled.

"Fine," came the muffled response.

Jack produced a small flashlight from his pants and looked through Carol's key ring. Gun walked to the woodpile next to his house and came back with a wedge-shaped splitting maul.

"This is ludicrous, it worked before," Carol said.

"Give me a little room," Gun said. He hefted the maul, swung it high, brought it down.

The lock broke under a single swing. Gun pulled the door open and stepped forward with Jack. It was black inside, and suddenly from the blackness sprang a heavy growl and the sharp snap of shell entering chamber. "Damn," whispered Gun.

Another voice said, "Lay it down, LaSalle."

Chapter 38

Jack bent slowly and laid the shotgun on the ground. Lyle Hedman stepped out from the shadows with a shotgun of his own, Rupert at his side. Three other men stepped forward and flanked Hedman, one on his right, two on his left. On the right was Horseley, one of the import guzzlers from two nights ago. Tonight he had a .45. Unholstered. The other two were unfamiliar to Gun. One was close to seven feet tall. He carried a shotgun too, and set a Coleman lantern on the ground. The third wore long, oily black hair, dark glasses, and held a .30-30 at the waist. It was aimed at Gun's midsection.

Hedman pointed at Gun's Remington, which still leaned against the boathouse wall. "Berg, get rid of that," he said. The big man, breathing heavily, took two steps back, picked up the shotgun, and broke it in half against the corner of the stone building.

"The maul, Pedersen," Lyle said.

Gun dropped the splitting maul on the ground. Rupert growled.

Hedman touched the dog's head. "It's okay, boy," he said, then turned and peered into the darkness. "Reverend? It's safe now." Almost immediately, Barr's lean face appeared over Hedman's shoulder.

"Old Samuel's a little nervous," said Lyle. He grinned broadly. "Surprised?"

"How did you know?" Carol said.

Geoff laughed and pushed his way between Jack and Mazy to stand at his father's side.

"Good work, Geoff," Lyle said. "Makes things a helluva lot neater."

"Simple job," Geoff said. He turned to Gun, winked. "I

179

got a pen from that cashier, the one in Hope. Wrote a note in the john on toilet paper. I put it on the toilet seat, right there where the next guy would see it. And it worked, damnit! I got the pen pretending I wanted cigarettes—"

"Smart of you, Geoff, now shut the hell up." Lyle's voice was trembling and the grin was gone from his face. "Gun, Jack, you guys made some hamburger out there in B.C. Congrats. Hope the war games were fun." He poked Gun in the chest with the barrel of the twelve-gauge. "You're a brave man, aren't you, Pedersen? You and your goddamn reputation. Sportsman. Lone wolf. Bullshit. Let me tell you how the public's gonna judge you now. They'll hear the name Gun Pedersen and they won't think Detroit Tigers. They'll think killer. And they'll be right. First degree, three counts. Guaranteed. I've got friends, and I've got witnesses. Jerry Drake, for one. He's the guy out there you didn't hit hard enough. Crawled off into the woods with just an egg on his head. Lucky. And there's Geoff, he was there. Barr, too. Remember the little conversation you and the reverend had before you flew off to Canada? Sunday morning, wasn't it? You told Barr just what you were planning to do. Told him you were going to kill me and Geoff and anyone else who stood between you and your daughter. You were in a frenzy, remember? Foaming at the mouth, screaming revenge. You were going goddamn nuts." Hedman looked over his shoulder at Barr. "Isn't that right, Reverend?"

Barr nodded, sober.

Gun said, "I guess we'll wait, see who the people believe."

Hedman shook his head and gripped one hand around the back of his neck, as if trying to work out a kink. "Shit," he said, "the people are only going to hear one story.

That'll make it easy."

It was silent for a few seconds, then Hedman laughed. "If you think I'm gonna let even one of you say one word to anyone about anything, you underestimate me." He leaned down and patted Rupert's head. "Gun, it's too bad you had to bring your friends into this. Because you've buried them."

Carol said, "People know the truth, Lyle. They've been reading my paper all day. We turn up dead and the party's over."

"That depends on how you die, Carol. We're talking boating accident here, plain and simple. You're on your way across the lake at night, sneaking into the county past the roadblocks, guilty as hell. Something happens and your boat goes down. It's a foggy night, you're going fast and careless, and down under Holliman's Bluff you run smack into Crazy Boy Rock." Hedman shifted the weight of his shotgun into the crook of an elbow and slapped his hands together. "And that's it," he said. "Remember Jimmy Latchfield and his wife. A terrible business, but what do you expect, skull hitting rock at thirty miles an hour." Hedman draped an arm around Geoff. "And of course, this guy'll survive to tell the story."

"Question for you," said Jack. "If we're as guilty as you say, then what the hell are we doing back here? How does Geoff explain that?"

Hedman licked his lips, tasted each detail. He threw a skinny arm around Barr's shoulders and hugged the grinning reverend close. "Geoff simply explains how you stole across the lake tonight for the purpose of getting rid of the man who could fill their story with holes. Shot poor Samuel Barr in the heart and then headed north again, only to barrel into Crazy Boy Rock and drown."

"Lyle?" Reverend Barr pulled away. His smile was frozen horror.

"There's too much riding on your ability to keep your nerve, Reverend. It's nothing personal."

"But we've been together on this from the start. You can trust me. My God!"

Hedman said, "Fraser—LaSalle's gun," and the man with the hair and dark glasses did as he was told. Lyle handed his own gun to the big man, Berg, then broke open Jack's over-and-under to be sure it was loaded.

"My God, Lyle!" Barr's voice had found a new, higher range. He folded his hands and held them up to Lyle in the manner of a formal greeting. "You're a fair man, you can't do this!"

Hedman jammed the end of the barrel into Barr's chest and backed him up. Barr nodded fast, as if agreeing to an order. His lips moved silently.

Gun said, "Lyle!" and took a step forward.

"Rupert!" Hedman ordered. The dog rose from the grass at Hedman's feet, compressed its body back into its hindquarters, then uncoiled into the air and shot straight toward Gun's face. Gun leaned forward and locked his elbows. With both hands he caught hold of Rupert's hard neck, the animal's driving weight backing him up a step. But he held fast. Rupert's claws slashed at Gun's face and arms and chest, and his teeth snapped like breaking ice. Gun found the animal's windpipe with his left hand and squeezed it with all the power he could force into his damaged fist. Then, holding the animal aloft with one arm, he speared his right hand through the dog's flailing legs and took firm hold on a rear thigh. He lifted Rupert high above his head. The dog twisted crazily and clawed at the sky, tail going round and round like the blade of a fan. Gun sucked his lungs full, exhaled a roar, and brought the dog spine first onto a bent knee. It sounded like the splitting of a great branch, and then Rupert was on the ground, spastic, jerking, twitching one foot, whining. His long body was bent the wrong way into a perfect vee, front and back legs pointing in opposite directions.

Hedman and Barr looked from Rupert to Gun, then at one another. Hedman raised the shotgun and put the barrel six inches from the minister's chest. An orange fire burst from the gun's mouth and the report was sharp yet muffled, like a firecracker under a heavy blanket. Reverend Barr hopped backward, raised a single finger, then fell to his side, and his head cracked against the stone boathouse.

Chapter 39

Carol bolted toward the fallen minister, but Fraser blocked her way, deer rifle in hand. Carol crossed her pale wrists in front of her breasts. Her slender fingers were spread wide. She turned and stared at Hedman. In the light from the Coleman lamp, Gun could see Carol's eyes blinking, a muscle ticking rhythmically in her jaw. She was working for control. That's right, Carol, Gun thought, keep a tight rein. He looked at Mazy, two steps to his left. She was staring at Hedman too, but self-possessed. She didn't even look surprised. Gun stepped toward her and took hold of her cool hand.

"You're over the edge, Lyle," Gun said quietly.

Lyle didn't answer. He was looking down at his dog, dead now. A fish jumped in the water not far off. Hedman's men watched their boss. Geoff stood stiff as a soldier.

Jack, on Gun's right, stood closest to the boathouse. Now he put an arm out and struck a leaning pose against the corner. The dead minister lay several feet in front of him. "Tell you what, Lyle." Jack's voice was so deep and loud in the silence that Hedman jerked. "You're going to find out what people think of you. There'll be an investigation, because people are going to demand it."

Hedman's face knotted up, went slack. He was panting like a man fresh from running eight flights of stairs. Gun looked at Jack, and their eyes met in a glimmer of understanding. Hedman was unlatched. There would be a way to take advantage of him, a way out—if everyone could just stay calm then move fast when the moment arrived.

Gun pulled Mazy close. "Geoff," he said, "do your old

man a favor and tell him it's over. Make a future for yourself, now while there's time."

Geoff turned to his father, who shivered once and looked around bright-eyed, like a man coming to. His eyes settled on Gun. "Shut up, Pedersen." He swung Jack's shotgun around like a pointing stick. "Okay, let's go. Berg, Fraser—get Pedersen's boat out of the shed and into the water. Horseley, help me keep an eye on these folks. Come on, get at it!"

Berg and Fraser rolled the boat down to the lake on its trailer and fiddled with the crank release as Hedman watched, glancing back a few times toward the bodies of Reverend Barr and Rupert.

"Shit," said Fraser, bending over the crank.

"Hurry it up!" Hedman said.

"It's stuck or something," Berg said.

"Then break it, asshole!" Lyle stormed over to the boat. "Here, lean on it, Berg. Put that fat to use. Move it!"

Whatever was stuck gave to Berg's weight, and soon they had the boat alongside the dock, and Fraser was yanking on the starter rope. The engine took hold, sputtered, and quit. Then started again.

"Good work," Gun said. "I haven't been able to get it going for weeks."

Hedman studied Gun out the corner of his eye then called out, "Keep that motor running, Fraser—hand on the throttle. Berg, bring me that medicine bag. Now."

Berg stepped from boat to dock and went to Hedman's side. He produced from his pocket a small bag resembling a shaving kit and handed it over. Lyle signaled for Geoff and passed him the shotgun, then he opened the bag and removed a syringe. He held it up before his face, the needle brilliant in the lamplight. "Gun, have you ever gone under the knife? How about you, Jack?" Hedman was yelling over the racket of the motor. "I have twice. And both times I thoroughly enjoyed the pre-operation bliss induced by this little baby." He waved the needle. "Straight from heaven, this stuff—but it so happens Berg here brought enough for just two injections, instead of the four like I told him, and you can probably guess who'll get them."

Gun squeezed Mazy's shoulder. He could feel her tension but knew she'd hold up. On the other side of Mazy, Jack was on one knee. He leaned forward, the schoolyard smile on his face again. His eyes were hard and sparkling.

Carol was seated on the ground, her mouth drawn flat. Under his breath Gun told her, "Things are going to happen fast. Get a good grip," and then Carol smiled, brave and accusatory.

"Okay," Lyle said, "I want you and you"—he pointed with his nose at Berg and Horseley—"to grab hold of the big man and keep him steady. These pinpricks hurt a little bit." Hedman flourished the needle. "Bring him right over here," he said.

Gun kissed Mazy on the cheek and then reached down to touch Carol's shoulder. He hoped she was ready. Berg and Horseley pushed him forward into the bright circle of lamplight, where Lyle's face looked thinner and sharper, lit as it was from below.

"Shirt off," Lyle said.

Gun took off the wool Pendleton and felt the chill air brighten his skin. Horseley tucked the .45 in his pants and locked both hands around Gun's right arm. Gun could feel the pitch of the man's nerves, tight as stretched wire. Berg was another matter, all that weight. The giant had his shotgun in his left hand, Gun's arm in his right. He was like something immovable, a piece of bedrock.

As Hedman knelt beside the lamp and fumbled with the bag, Gun measured distances. Straight ahead thirty feet, Fraser and his sunglasses sat in the Alumacraft, playing the throttle, deer rifle close by. Geoff stood a few yards to Gun's left; Jack, Carol, and Mazy were on his right. Geoff had the gun butted against his hip and pointed at Jack, but Gun doubted he'd use it. No barrels on Gun.

Hedman said, "Okay," then stood up, the needle ready. "Relax now, be brave," he crooned.

Horseley and Berg tightened down. "Jack," Gun said, "I guess this is it."

Jack nodded and blinked. Gun saw his friend's hand close around a baseball-sized rock next to his knee. Hedman stepped to Gun's side. "Keep him there, boys," he said.

Gun tensed. The icy sphere expanding beneath his heart was so light and buoyant he felt it might lift him off the ground. He watched for the glint of the needle. Saw it. *Now.*

Chapter 40

He released himself into motion, clamped the fingers of his right hand on Horseley's belt, and used his own weight as a fulcrum. Horseley came up like a feed sack over Gun's shoulder and into Hedman's face. The needle flew. Berg lifted his shotgun but Gun brought up his knee, and the giant bent double over a ruined groin. Gun sprinted for the boat. He was three strides back of Jack, one behind Mazy and Carol. Geoff was on the ground, a red lump growing under one eye.

Fraser was still in the boat, and Gun saw Jack get there first—rifle fire lighting the air—and launch a flying cross-body. Then Fraser's feet were pointing up and his body was hitting the water and Jack was yelling "stay low" and throwing the women into the bottom of the boat. Gun freed the tie-line and jumped. Jack throttled wide open and swung the bow into the fog. Gun couldn't see more than fifty feet ahead.

"Damn this motor!" Jack yelled. He had it full throttle and was messing with the lean-rich dial, trying to coax out more power. Mazy and Carol lay in the center of the boat, and Gun sat on the rear seat next to Jack, their weight pulling the bow off the water for speed.

Behind them the headlight beam of Young's runabout swung like a long pole across the water, then flared into a spot.

"The islands," Gun said.

The town of Stony was five miles south, too far, but the cluster of islands lay a mile due west and offered sanctuary: small bays lined with overhanging limbs, abandoned cabins, caves in washed-out shorelines. If they could beat them to the islands, they might elude him till morning.

A rifle shot rang across the water and whined overhead. Gun and Jack slid off the seat to the floor. Jack kept his hand on the stick and his head just high enough to hold a straight line. The runabout was coming on in a hurry—Gun could already make out the silhouettes of the men on board. Five of them. A second shot ripped into the stern, not a foot from Gun's face.

The islands were a couple hundred yards off when the big boat came roaring up alongside, and Berg raised himself over the windshield, shotgun in hand. Jack threw the Alumacraft into a steep bank then straightened out again, but the runabout stayed on them. Again Berg positioned for a shot, and again Jack banked, this time in the other direction. Berg fired. The shot was like thunder, and pellets sprayed the boat's high-riding side. Jack kept the port gunwale running flush on the water, starboard high in the air, and he scribed a tight circle on the water. Horseley followed, drawing a close line around them. They were near enough for Gun to see Geoff's bloodied face at Berg's shoulder. After two three-sixties, Jack rammed the stick all the way over, and the bow lurched around like the arm of a crane, and broke off in a wild tangent directly toward the broadside of the runabout. On impact, the bow of the Alumacraft split wide open, and the little boat stood up on the water, proud as a pine tree.

Gun landed free of the wreckage. When he surfaced, his boat was lying behind him, upside down on the lake. Ahead, the runabout's light bent toward him in a fast arc, coming hard. He couldn't tell if anyone was still in it. Then in the boat's lighted path he saw the head of a swimmer, heard a loud thump as the head went down before the charging prow. He dove deep, heart crashing in his ears.

The boat passed overhead and Gun surfaced. He swam hard toward the bobbing lump, not allowing himself to think. Somewhere behind there was splashing, a man's scream, a low grunt that sounded like Jack. He reached the floating body in a dozen fast strokes. The head was face-down, long hair fanning out, skull cleft like a notched melon. No blood, only sharp white bone and spongy-looking brain. Gun lifted the face and looked into the staring eyes of Fraser. His sunglasses covered his mouth.

"Thank God," Gun whispered. "Mazy! Jack! Carol!" he yelled. No answer. Just more splashing, labored breathing, a curse, the sounds seeming to come from behind the turtled Alumacraft. Gun swam toward it, then stopped at the sound of the runabout—it was swinging toward him again, slowly this time, and Lyle Hedman stood at the wheel. The boat had a gash in the middle of port side, well above the waterline.

Gun kept his arms and legs moving steadily and held his head low, preparing to dive again, when a face popped up in front of the tipped Alumacraft. Jack? He couldn't tell. The boat's light came closer and sharpened his vision. It was Horseley in the water, and his eyes were fastened on Gun. The headlight moved in. Gun saw Horseley's .45 on the surface of the lake, saw the small round hole of the barrel. Then a shadow appeared from behind him and a line of bright silver flashed beneath Horseley's chin. A stream of blood arced from his neck. The shadow withdrew beneath the boat. Horseley slipped out of sight. Gun locked air in his chest and dove away from the runabout, remembering the fish-cleaning knife.

Carol.

Hedman's shotgun boomed. Pellets hit the water and rattled off the aluminum hull of the capsized boat. Gun dove deep and pushed hard for the sound of Hedman's slowing motor. He kicked his feet violently, thrust his arms forward and back, forward and back. His lungs burned. The runabout was barely moving now, the engine idling, and Gun swam beneath it and came up on the other side, sucked his lungs full without making a sound. He fastened his fingers on the gunwale and pulled down with everything he had. The boat rocked hard and Hedman fell toward the rear, managing to hang onto his shotgun but landing facefirst in the twisted snarls of anchor rope.

Gun vaulted over the side and landed on hip and elbow beneath the steering wheel and throttle lever. Hedman tossed off coils of rope and pushed to his knees. Both men reached their feet at the same moment. Hedman—eight feet away, a circle of rope hanging from his neck—held the shotgun at his waist, barrel toward Gun's chest.

Jamming the throttle lever to full power, Gun threw himself free of the boat. Hedman flipped backward into the lake, blasting a red hole in the sky. Gun swam toward him as the boat charged away. He reached him, put a hand on his shoulder, then Lyle's neck popped like a cork and the rope yanked him into the air. The motor roared a moment's resistance and then Lyle was gone, horizontal on the water, flying, arms and legs bouncing on the surface of the lake like empty cans thrown from a speeding car. He was heading straight for town.

Gun swam toward the wreckage of his old boat. He couldn't hear the splashing anymore. "Mazy!" he called.

"Dad!"

He tried to pinpoint her voice. It came again. "Dad!" Then he saw her, swimming toward him in the foggy darkness. She had two heads.

"Mazy . . ."

Now he saw she was swimming arm-in-arm with Jack, helping and being helped, the two of them negotiating a sort of double sidestroke. Jack's face ran with blood. Gun met them beside the capsized boat, at the place where Horseley had gone under.

"You're all right?" Gun said.

Jack was breathing hard, but he forced a smile and showed Gun a new black space in his top row of teeth. "Wouldn't be, if your girl hadn't clubbed that caveman with an oar. He was too much for me. Hell, it was like trying to drown an island."

"He got away, took off swimming in that direction," said Mazy, pointing. Then her eyes went black with fear. "Where's Carol?"

"Carol's fine, I believe. Isn't that right, Carol?" Gun said, lifting his voice.

A soft splash sounded from underneath the boat, and Carol surfaced between Mazy and Gun. Wet hair covered her face like a striped mask. Gun pushed the hair from her eyes and lifted her right arm into the air. In her fist she held the fish-cleaning knife with the slender, curving blade.

Chapter 41

Two days later, Thursday morning, seven o'clock. The sun was clean white and shining through the trees. A storm had passed through in the night, purifying the air. Gun finished his morning swim and walked ashore. He was wearing only a pair of gray longjohns. Stony Lake was still very cold. He took a towel from where it hung on a dock post and dried his chest and shoulders. He was rubbing his hair dry when he heard Carol's voice.

"Still in your longies, I see."

He looked up and saw her in the outfield grass. Even from twenty yards he could tell her green eyes were rested. Her black hair shone. Beside her was her son Michael, whom Gun had met the day before. He had his mother's long legs and someone else's face, a rugged face, wide cheekbones, a bony nose. Gun joined them on the grass and shook hands with Michael.

"We've got some news," Carol said. "They found Berg, and Geoff too." Berg and Geoff had been the only two unaccounted for since the other night. The search had been large and well-publicized.

"Together, were they?" asked Gun.

"Far from it. Berg was hiding in Nick Faris's barn, up in the haymow. State police bloodhounds found him last night about eleven-thirty." Carol touched Gun's arm. "We'd better get you inside, you've got goose bumps."

"What about Geoff?"

Michael put an arm around his mother's shoulders. Carol said, "Geoff washed up on the town beach. Early this morning."

Gun turned toward the lake. He pictured Geoff's face, bloated and pale, forced it from his mind.

After a moment Carol said, "Michael and I were wondering if you and Mazy would like to go out, get some breakfast."

Gun laughed. "Can't you smell it?" Carol and Michael put their noses in the air. "That's Mazy's bacon frying," he said.

***

Four plates of bacon, eggs, and hash browns later, they sat at Gun's table sipping coffee. Yesterday they'd all been obliged to tell their stories again and again—to investigators from the FBI and the state crime bureau, to media folks of every stripe. Mazy had phoned an exclusive to the *Minneapolis Tribune*, which had appeared this morning under a headline an inch tall. Today was a breather.

There had been several minutes of silence when someone belted Gun's door, boom boom boom, and an enormous voice bawled, "Gun Pedersen, you home?"

Mike blinked at his mom, who lifted her shoulders. Mazy said, "Beats me." Gun smiled, took a long plug of coffee and stood from the table, stepped outside.

Bowser was clean-shaven and round-headed, grinning. The bottom several buttons of his red flannel shirt were missing and his big hairy belly looked like somebody's naked rear end backing out of a tent. "Went into that cutesy barber shop of Loretta's last night," he said. Behind them a celebration of summer birds swirled in the white pines. "Went in and sat down and told them, I don't want bald but I want its first cousin."

"You're improved," Gun said.

"Talk in town is all Gun Pedersen," Bowser said.

"Great."

"You done a job on 'em," said Bowser. His left eye held respectfully on Gun's face while the right went wandering toward the lake. "Done a job on Hedman, may he fry. Done a job on the old Loon Mall. I admire that, Gun."

"Come in for breakfast."

"Naw. You got folks over." Bowser stood in the bird-wild noise of the morning, hands in his pockets, breathing easily. A swell of far-off laughter came from the house, Mazy and Carol and Mike.

"I felt real bad about missing your dad's funeral," Gun said. "I thought about it a lot that day."

Bowser shifted his weight from one thick leg to the other, shot a stream of saliva to the ground. "Hard to be in two places at once. And you didn't miss a hell of a lot. Arnie Quinn at the funeral parlor don't waste no time. A couple of tunes and a prayer, and Arnie and his helper roll 'em right out to the limo. Best thing about it all was taps at the graveyard. That trumpet player, now, he knew how to make a pretty sound. I loved that."

They were quiet. Bowser took one hand from his pocket and peeked at the dirt under his nails, then looked evenly at Gun. His eyes almost seemed to focus on the same point, nearly came together to function as a matched pair. "You're welcome at the home place, Gun. Anytime."

"Thanks."

The kitchen was relaxed and gold with sun when Gun stepped back inside. Mike was leaning into the fridge, reading a buttermilk carton. Mazy rested back in her chair, eyes closed. Carol folded the newspaper she held and looked a question at Gun. He raised his arms and held them out from his sides, palms up.

"Happy day," he said.

BOOKS IN THIS SERIES

The Gun Pedersen Series

Comeback

After the tragic death of his wife and in the midst of scandal, six-foot-six Gunsten Pedersen—the Detroit Tigers' powerful, veteran home-run hitter—walked away from the sport that he loved. Fleeing the disappointed fans and the coldhearted press, he retired to the tranquil solitude of Minnesota's north woods. But a millionaire real estate investor is out to tear the countryside apart. The townspeople are divided, and Gun is pulled into the center of the storm when his daughter becomes a pawn in a campaign that's turned vicious. Pedersen must go to bat for everything he holds dear—and this game may cost him his life.

Swing

Gunsten Pedersen knew about baseball and death. A tragedy took the former slugger out of the majors, and the only diamonds he sees now are the stars shining in the cold North Woods night. That is, until Miles Gates— an old friend in big trouble—calls Gun down to Florida. What he finds there is a trail of brutal killings, some aging ballplayers, shady characters, and the beautiful sister of a reporter who died for his story. Gun discovers the truth behind the murder spree, and he strikes at it as hard as he ever hit a fastball in his prime. But in the warmth of the Florida sun, old dreams and old hatreds have a way of coming back to life. When Gun returns north, so does a man who wants him dead.

Strike

When gold is discovered near reservation land in Minnesota, Gunsten Pedersen becomes enmeshed in a stand-off between a gold mining company and the Ojibwe tribe. Innocent people are murdered, and Gun must navigate the gray zone between white and Native-American worlds.

Sacrifice

In the late 1960s, two young men left a small Michigan town. One was Gunsten Pedersen, who went on to a career with the Detroit Tigers. The other was Harry Summers, a gifted infielder who disappeared from Copper Strike on a rainy June night. Now an excavation crew has unearthed Harry's bones, and with them, grim evidence of murder—a hammer imbedded in Harry's skull. Gun Pedersen, hometown hero turned recluse, has returned for Harry's funeral. But when evidence of the decades-old crime points to Gun's father, Gun is caught in a tragedy from Copper Strike's past. With his own wedding only days away, Gun is finding some hard and wrenching truths: about the things fathers do for sons, about the things you can't ever leave behind, and about a killer who has yet one more life to take.

The Sinners' League

When a friend turns up dead in Minneapolis, victim of an

ugly murder, Gunsten Pedersen must leave his sanctuary on Stony Lake in northern Minnesota and immerse himself in the dirty underworld of human trafficking.

Hard Curves

When Gunsten Pedersen witnesses the murder of a minor-league ballplayer in Duluth, Minnesota, he is drawn into a blackmail scheme involving an aging baseball groupie and the corrupt owner of a big-league franchise.

BOOKS BY THE AUTHORS

<u>The Gun Pedersen Series, by Leif Enger and Lin Enger:</u>

Comeback
Swing
Strike
Sacrifice
The Sinners' League
Hard Curves

<u>Novels by Leif Enger:</u>

Peace Like a River
So Brave, Young, and Handsome
Virgil Wander
I Cheerfully Refuse

<u>Novels by Lin Enger:</u>

Undiscovered Country
The High Divide
American Gospel

13025403R00118